Red River Deep

CAROLYN BROWN

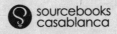
sourcebooks
casablanca

Published by Sourcebooks Casablanca, an imprint of Sourcebooks
P.O. Box 4410, Naperville, Illinois 60567-4410
(630) 961-3900
sourcebooks.com

Originally published as *This Time Forever* in 1997 in the United States of America by Precious
Gems, an imprint of Kensington. This edition issued based on *Red River Deep*, published
in 2014 in the United States of America by Vintage, an imprint of Folio Unbound.

Printed and bound in the United States of America.
OPM 10 9 8 7 6 5 4 3 2 1

This one is for Deb Werksman with many thanks!

Dear Readers,

When I started dusting this book off for a reissue, I was amazed at how much had changed in the past twenty-five years. When I look at pictures of my family from the year the original copy of this book came out, I'm shocked—and even more so when I see a photo of Mr. B and myself. One thing that is comforting is that, although we now have cell phones and all this fancy technology, love is still the same as it has been since the beginning of time. And sometimes folks get a second chance at it, even when they've made mistakes and blown the first try.

I have a lot of folks to thank for their help in doing this job. Thanks to my agency, Folio Management, and to my agent, Erin Niumata, for everything they do. Thanks to Sourcebooks and Deb Werksman for working with me on this new edition, and to all my readers for their support and love through the past years and through more than a hundred books. And thanks to my husband, Mr. B, who is my biggest supporter! All of you deserve a standing ovation.

I enjoyed going back to the beginning of my career and inviting the characters to take up residence in my heart and mind—it was like a family reunion with old friends. I hope you feel the same way when you read the last chapter.

Until next time,
Carolyn Brown

Chapter 1

AUSTIN JERKED HIS T-SHIRT OVER HIS HEAD HARD ENOUGH to split the seams over his broad shoulders. He combed his dark-brown hair with his fingertips, picked up his worn blue duffel bag, kicked a pile of dirty clothes out of his way, and headed for the living room door.

"Austin, don't you dare walk out that door. It's pouring rain and it's turning to sleet. I'll take you back to the dorm even if you are pigheaded and hateful." Tracey came out of the bedroom hopping on her right foot while she tried desperately to get a high-top athletic shoe on her left. She had slipped on a T-shirt, but she wasn't wearing a bra and her jeans were still unzipped.

Austin scowled at her. "Ever consider untying the laces before you put them on?" he asked in a slow Texas drawl without a bit of warmth in his tone. This wasn't a new fight but just another version of one that they'd had too many times to count. "You can't put on your own shoes"—he threw up his hands in desperation—"and you can't even pick up your own clothes. Your daddy spends a fortune on your college education, but you take it all for granted."

Tracey jerked the high-top onto her foot and glared at him. "Just go get in the car and quit preaching at me." Her voice was low and husky, telling Austin that she was on the verge of another one of what his grandmother called an out-and-out "hissy fit" that would end in tears, but tonight he didn't care. He'd had enough, and they both needed a break from each other. He slung the apartment door open with enough force that the hinges creaked. Then he stomped out to Tracey's bright-red Camaro and folded his six-foot frame into the passenger seat.

She followed him, dashing through the driving rain and sleet to her car, and slid behind the wheel.

"Austin, I just don't understand why you're so angry." She jammed the key into the ignition and turned on the engine. "All I want is for you to come home with me for three days and spend Christmas with me and my father. I'm beginning to think you're not serious about me." Her voice cracked.

"Don't start that." Austin stared out the front window, refusing to look at her for even a second. He would lose all resolve if she started to cry. "Just don't. You know I love you, but I have to work during winter break. My daddy didn't give me a bank account to spend as I please."

"It's just three days. I'll write you a check for whatever you would make those days," Tracey said.

"Ouch! There went the rest of my manhood," Austin said. "If I don't show up for work, I'll lose my job. I have to be back at the factory on Monday morning after Christmas. I need the money, Trace. You don't know what it means to have to work your way through college, and I don't know how to make you understand."

Austin glanced over at her, expecting tears, but what he saw was a stone-cold glare. "If it's so almighty important to you that I meet your daddy, why don't you cancel your skiing trip and stay home on Christmas Eve and Christmas, and bring your father out to the ranch to meet me and my folks? Those are the only two days that I don't have to work during break."

"We don't get to spend New Year's Eve together?" Tracey asked. "I'll be home by then."

Austin shook his head. "I promised the floor boss that

I'd work New Year's Eve and New Year's Day. They need the help and I need the overtime, and since I get to be off Christmas, it only seems fair."

He looked out the window at the pouring rain but he couldn't see anything. "This is like us right now, Trace. We're together, but nothing is clear."

Tracey reached across the console and cupped his chin in her hand. "Look at me, Austin. We've got to compromise if we're going to have a relationship."

"Compromise means that we each give a little. I've been doing ninety percent of the giving, and you've been doing one hundred percent of the taking," he said.

"It's not my fault that I don't have to work. My daddy can't help being generous. I'm his only child. It doesn't mean I'm—"

"Spoiled?" He finished the sentence for her. "Yes, Tracey, you are, but I love you in spite of that. Just don't expect me to drop everything, including my job, to do what you want." He stared into her bright-green eyes, and his voice softened. "You've had everything handed to you, Trace. And you take it all for granted. I'm just asking that you respect the fact that I have to work."

"Oh, sure." Tracey dropped her hands. She put the car in

reverse and backed out so fast that the tires skidded on the slick pavement. "I know what's really on your mind. You're afraid. The only reason you won't go home with me is that you're scared to meet my daddy."

Austin had been in love with Tracey from the day they'd met two years ago. He'd seen her sitting alone in the student lounge, taking up a whole booth with sheaves of notes and open textbooks, evidently trying to write a paper. Red hair fell down her back to her curvy waist, and when she'd looked up at him, Austin had gotten lost in the greenest eyes he'd ever seen.

"Can I help you with something?" Tracey had asked.

"No, but maybe I can help you," he had answered. "Is that a Comp I assignment you're working on?" He pointed at the textbook lying on the table in front of her.

"Yes." She had smiled and the whole room lit up.

"I took that class last semester with Dr. Hinson. What's your topic? Mind if I sit down?" Without even closing his eyes, he could visualize her sitting there in a T-shirt she must've gotten at a Blake Shelton concert and a pair of jeans that hugged every curve.

"I haven't decided on a topic. Got any ideas?" she had asked.

"How about writing an essay on your first days of college and how your opinion has changed now that you've got half a semester done?" he asked. "That's something I wrote about, and I got an A on the paper."

After that day, they'd been inseparable.

"What are you thinking about so hard?" she asked as she drove down University Boulevard and made a left turn into Southeastern Oklahoma State University and toward his dorm room. She always drove too fast, but if anger could be measured in miles per hour over the speed limit, she was right on the edge of one of her famous hissy fits.

"The first day we met," he answered.

"It was love at first sight." She smiled.

"Yes, it was," he agreed, "but being in love isn't easy."

"It would be if you would move in with me," she said. "But you've got to be stubborn about money."

"Think about it," he said, sighing. "When we have one of these arguments, we need our own space. We aren't ready to move in together."

———————

Why does he really have to be so stubborn and full of pride? Tracey fumed.

She wasn't asking for the moon. She just wanted three days—that's all. Three days away from school and tests and work. The semester had ended, and they deserved a much-needed break. *He's right. You do need your own space.* Her father's voice popped into her head.

Don't take up for him, she argued. *I'm your daughter. You're supposed to be on my side, and besides, you've been bugging me for weeks to bring him to Purcell so you can meet him.*

Tears hung on her lashes, but she blinked them away. She wouldn't let Austin see her cry—no, sir! Not this time. If he wanted to work, then by damn, he could go to his factory job where he picked stuff off shelves and got it loaded up to go out to stores all over the nation. She was going home for the holidays and then she was off for a skiing trip in Colorado with her friends, like she did every year. She braked hard and brought her car to a sliding stop in front of his dorm.

"Is there anything I can do to make you change your mind?" she asked.

Austin shook his head. "No, there's not, Tracey. My family is waiting to serve Christmas dinner until four o'clock just so I can be there with them. Even if I could get off work, which I can't, I wouldn't. Why don't you go home with me for the holiday season? There's lots of room in the farmhouse, and they would love to have you."

She shook her head. Her father would be alone, and Christmas meant a lot to him, plus her friends would never forgive her if she didn't go with them to Colorado.

"Listen to me for once, Trace. Really listen. I love you Red River deep but right now you and I need some coolin'-off time to see what we want out of life." His voice cracked. "Let's have a break for this month that we're out of school."

"Kind of like Ross and Rachel on *Friends*?" she asked. "You know how that ended, so why don't we just say goodbye now and be done with it? Go on back to your precious farm in Tom Bean, Texas. Find you one of those country girls who are happy staying home and making their big, tough men happy."

"Maybe I'll do just that, Trace." Austin opened the car door and slung one of his long legs out. "And you can drive home in this red toy your daddy bought you and go huntin' for a guy who can afford to hire a dozen maids to pick up after you. I'm sure as hell not goin' to do it."

Austin grabbed his duffel bag from the back seat and uncurled his body from inside the sports car. He slammed the car door behind him and stomped off toward the dorm without even a backward glance.

Tracey beat her palms on the steering wheel in helpless fury until they ached and the diamond in the little promise ring Austin had given her for their two-year anniversary caught her attention. She jerked it off her finger and tossed it into the back seat. Then she remembered the gold pendant with his initials that hung from an expensive chain around her neck. She curled her fingers around the necklace that he'd given her for their six-month anniversary and gave the necklace a hard tug. Several of the links broke, but she didn't care. She threw it over her shoulder and started to sob.

"You want a break?" Tears streamed down her cheeks. "Well, you can damn well have one, Austin. You can go back to your Podunk hometown with the silly name and work all holiday. I hope you are miserable every single minute." She put the car in reverse and started to back away from the curb.

A delivery truck honked, startling her so badly that she braked hard. The truck's headlights filled her rearview mirror and she just knew it was going to rear-end her, but it slid to a stop within what looked like a hairsbreadth. The driver laid on the horn for a full minute, which didn't help her racing heart one single bit.

"Hold on!" she screamed as she eased ahead at a snail's pace. Tracey had known from the day that Austin helped her with her English Comp paper that she was going to fall in love with him. He was tall, dark, and handsome, and sweet, funny, and kind. All the things she liked in a guy, but then he was also stubborn and neat—two things that drove her crazy.

They were on a break, weren't they? Did that mean he would be waiting by the phone for her to call him and apologize? Or would he send her a text the next morning and say he was sorry?

"Well, I'm not calling him," she muttered. "As Daddy says, I'll trade my front seat in heaven for a back seat in hell on a barbed-wire fence before I call up Mr. Austin Nelson Miller to apologize."

Tracey pulled over into a doughnut store's parking lot to let the truck go past her. Lights were on in the store, but it wouldn't open for another two hours—not until five o'clock. If it had been open, she would have gone inside and bought a box full of pastries. Anger always made her hungry, and she was just about to the point of downing half a dozen apple fritters and polishing that off with three or four maple-glazed long johns. She eased out onto the road again and drove straight to her apartment complex.

There was no way to go from the car to her front door without getting wet, but she took off in a dead run from the car and down the sidewalk. She had only gone a few feet when her feet went out from under her, and she sat down in an ice-cold puddle. Her purse flew off to one side and dumped everything out.

They put a zipper on that expensive handbag for a reason. Austin's voice was so clear that she looked over her shoulder to see if he had followed her home.

She scrambled around to get her wallet, phone, and sunglasses all put back in her purse. "If we're on a break, then you don't get to pop into my head. Go away."

Once inside her place, she went straight to the bathroom, stripped out of her wet clothing and left them lying on the floor, and then wrapped a second towel around her body. Matilda, the lady who cleaned for her each week, would be there tomorrow so Tracey waded through the pile of wet things and headed straight for the bedroom. She dropped the towel, put on a pair of flannel pajama bottoms and a tank top, and threw herself on the bed. Wrapping her arms around the pillow where Austin had laid his head just a little while ago, she inhaled deeply. Tomorrow when she went home, she would take the pillowcase with her—and when she returned from her trip to the mountains, she would call him.

Before daybreak the next morning, Austin threw his packed bags into the bed of his pickup truck, a vintage Chevrolet Silverado that had enough dents to give it personality, but the motor hummed like a brand-new model when he turned the ignition on. He'd never cared that the upholstery had worn out on the big, bench-style front seat. Grandma had given him one of her quilts to spread over the seat, and unlike Tracey's fancy little car with a console separating them, when they went somewhere in his truck—which wasn't very often—she could sit right next to him.

He slid behind the wheel, slammed the door, and drove back home to Tom Bean, Texas, getting there in time to sit down with his parents for breakfast.

"Hey, you're early!" His mother, Ellie, met him halfway across the room and hugged him. A tall woman with blond chin-length hair, she had the same bright-blue eyes that Austin had.

"What's wrong, Son?" his father, Andrew, asked. "You look like you just lost your best friend."

Looking at his father always reminded Austin of what he himself would look like in thirty years. His father's dark hair had gray streaks, and wrinkles had gathered around his steely blue-gray eyes.

"Tracey and I are on a break for the holidays." Austin

took a plate from the cabinet and silverware from a drawer and carried them to the table.

"Maybe it's for the best." Ellie brought out a jar of strawberry jam from the refrigerator and put it beside Austin's plate. "I saved back one jar of what I made last spring for when you came home this month. And about Tracey, you've been dating her for two years, and she's always got an excuse not to meet your family, not even when we come up to Durant to see you."

"Absence makes the heart grow fonder," Andrew said.

"I hope so." Austin pulled out a chair and sat down. "I love her, but…"

"As long as there's a 'but,' you need to be careful," Andrew told him. "When it's real love, there won't be a single 'but.'"

"You need time to think things through." Ellie took her seat and passed the biscuits over to Austin. "Have some breakfast. You'll think better on a full stomach."

"Hard work helps too," Andrew said.

"Need some wood chopped?" Austin asked. "I don't go in to work today until four o'clock."

"We can always use more wood stacked up at the end of the house," Andrew said, "but I had a mind to stretch some new barbed wire around the north pasture."

"Count me in." Austin split two biscuits, laid them on his plate, and covered them with sausage gravy.

━━━━━━━━━

Tracey awoke to sunrays pouring in her window and warming her face the next morning. She glanced over at the clock and was surprised to see that it was already after nine o'clock. Her father was expecting her to meet him at Ruby's that day for lunch, and it was a two-hour drive. She didn't have to worry about packing since she kept clothing and all her toiletries in both places, but she did need to take a shower and get dressed.

At a quarter to ten, she walked out the door of her messy apartment. When she returned in a month, Matilda would have it all tidied up and the refrigerator cleaned out. Tracey made a mental note to send her a grocery list so she could have the pantry and freezer stocked as well. Austin liked strawberry jam, and he loved omelets, so she would add eggs and jam to the list.

Why would you do that? the pesky voice in her head asked. *He might enjoy this break so much that he doesn't want to get back together with you.*

"We fight. We make up," Tracey said as she hit the remote

button to open her car and crossed the well-manicured lawn. The rain had beaten the pansies down, but some of them were lifting their purple faces up to the sun. "We're tough like those little winter flowers. We'll make it." She got into her car and got to her father's favorite little diner at the same time he did.

"Perfect timing," her father, Frank, said as he crawled out of his late-model Ford pickup truck. "How did you do this semester?"

"All A's but one B in math." She met her father between the two vehicles and hugged him tightly. "I guess I got Mama's math skills instead of yours."

Her dad was about the same height as Tracey's five feet ten inches and had the same red hair that she did, but his eyes were a deep mossy green, and Tracey's were mossy green, like her mother's had been. Austin said they were just a little lighter than the water in the Red River and that they mesmerized him.

"Your mother"—Frank chuckled—"was amazing at her job, but she couldn't even balance a checkbook. I'd say you got a mix of both of us. Let's go get a chicken-fried steak, and you can tell me why your eyes look so sad."

"I'm fine, Daddy," Tracey said.

"Your words say one thing. Those pretty brown eyes that you got from your mother tell a different story. She would have made a terrible poker player. Whatever she was thinking came right through on her face." Frank opened the door for Tracey and stood to one side.

The waitress seated them at a booth and laid two menus on the table.

"Two of your Wednesday specials," Frank said.

"Chicken-fried steaks, mashed potatoes, green beans." The lady talked as she made notes on her order pad. "Want to change the sides?"

"Not for me," Frank said. "But I would like a tall glass of sweet tea and an order of fried green tomatoes for an appetizer."

"I'd like sweet potato fries and broccoli, and sweet tea to drink also," Tracey said.

The woman nodded and rushed off to wait on another customer.

"No promise ring," Frank said. "No necklace?"

"We're on a break this whole month. He's so damned stubborn, Daddy." Tracey sighed.

"Why?" Frank asked.

"I just told you." She sighed again. "He's so stubborn. I

wanted him to come to Purcell for three days at Christmas. It's not like I was asking him to not work the whole month, and he wouldn't do it."

"Maybe it's for the best," Frank said. "Time apart will be good for both of you. It always is, and, honey, when he's ready for us to meet each other, it will happen. Don't rush things."

"What if it's one of those out-of-sight, out-of-mind things, Daddy?" Tracey asked. "I love him."

Frank reached across the table and patted her hand. "Things tend to work out the way they're supposed to. I've got flowers out there in the truck. After lunch, I thought we'd go to the cemetery and put them on your mother's grave."

"I'd like that, Daddy. Even after all these years, I still miss her so much." Tracey managed a weak smile.

Chapter 2

"CAN WE GET YOU ANYTHING?" LIZZY ASKED TRACEY.

"I'll stay inside with you," Sarah offered.

"I've just eaten something wrong," Tracey assured them. "We're only here a couple more days. Y'all get out there on the slopes and have a good time. I'll be fine by morning. I've got a whole pot of chamomile tea, a blaze in the fireplace, and this sexy book to keep me company."

"If you're sure?" Lizzy eyed the tram coming up to the lodge.

"Positive." Tracey nodded even though she felt like she would have to make another trip to the bathroom any minute. "Go! Bring me back stories of how handsome the ski instructors are."

"Won't be as sexy as your Austin." Sarah pulled her

stocking cap down over her golden-blond hair. "When are you ever going to bring him home for us to meet?"

"Workin' on it," Tracey said. "With y'all both out in California studying to be actors, our schedules don't cross nearly often enough."

"Amen to that," Lizzy said. "You should come to LA for spring break and maybe bring him with you."

"Oh, no!" Tracey forced a smile. "As sexy as he is, y'all would grab him up to play the lead part in some blockbuster movie. Now get out of here before you miss the tram."

Two days later, she still felt and looked like hell when the three girls said goodbye at the airport. Lizzy and Sarah's flight to LA left an hour before Tracey's, and she spent most of that time hugging one of the toilets in a stall in the ladies' room.

This isn't fair, she thought when she heard the boarding call for her flight to Oklahoma City. *I didn't even drink, and I've got a hangover.*

Like she'd done several times a day for the past three weeks, she checked her phone a dozen times during the hour she was in the air, but there was nothing, not a single word from Austin. Her father waited for her at the baggage check and frowned when he saw her.

"You look like hell," Frank said.

"It's just a stomach bug," she told him as she pulled her bright-red suitcase off the conveyor belt. "I thought it was the shrimp we had the first day we were there, but it's hanging on too long to have been that."

Frank took the bag from her and rolled it outside. "My truck is right across the street. I snagged a good spot. Please tell me that you haven't made yourself sick over Austin not calling."

"I have not," Tracey said with enough conviction that she almost convinced herself.

"Good," Frank said. "Molly is making chicken and dumplings because she knows it's your favorite."

"Bless her heart." Tracey appreciated the housekeeper/ nanny/surrogate grandmother that Molly was and hoped to hell she was able to keep the dumplings down.

When they were back home, Frank carried Tracey's suitcase up the winding staircase to her bedroom. He set it on the bench at the foot of her king-size bed and gave Tracey a hug. "I've got to go to the office and tie up some loose ends, but I'll be back by suppertime."

"I'll save you some dumplings," she said.

"See that you do." Frank smiled.

He had barely cleared the room when her phone rang.

She slung her purse off her shoulder, dumped all the contents on the bed, and grabbed the cell phone before it rang the third time. Without even looking at the caller ID, she slid the button across to answer the call.

"Hello!" she said.

"You sound a little more chipper than you did when we left you," Lizzy said. "We're stuck at Dallas. Snow and ice. Looks like we won't be home until tomorrow."

Tracey stretched out on her bed. "You should have come home with me," she said. "It's cold, but the sun is shining here in Purcell, and Molly is making dumplings."

Lizzy groaned. "I don't like you right now."

Tracey giggled. "Call me when you get home?"

"Of course," Lizzy said. "Sarah is motioning to me that our table is ready. Glad you made it back. Keep in touch."

"Will do. Bye now." Tracey ended the call and tossed the phone over on the pillow beside her.

She lay there for a few minutes and picked up the phone again. She called Molly's number, and the older woman answered on the first ring.

"Are you home?" Molly asked. "Sorry I wasn't there. I had to make a run to the grocery store and to the cleaners for your father."

"Molly, did I get any mail while I was gone?"

"Honey, I don't remember anything coming other than maybe some late Christmas cards, but it's all on the sideboard there in the foyer," Molly said.

"Thanks, Molly. See you in a little while." Tracey was already on her feet and headed out of her room when she said goodbye and ended the call.

She hurried down the stairs and rifled through the envelopes in the basket on the sideboard. Bills for her credit cards, addressed to her father, Frank Walker. Tracey tossed them aside without opening them. A long envelope from her apartment complex's office...probably the bill for the next six months' rent. A dozen Christmas cards from friends, but nothing from Austin.

The room started spinning, and she sat down on the bottom step before she fainted. She put her head between her knees and sucked up gulps of air. This was crazy. The love of her life hadn't called, sent a text, or even mailed a Christmas card, but he would come around. He'd told her a million times that he loved her Red River deep, and that kind of love didn't stop because of some silly argument.

Molly found Tracey still sitting there when she came in the front door. She set a bag of groceries on the sideboard and eased down beside Tracey. "You don't look good, darlin' girl. You're pale as a ghost, and you look like you could start crying any minute. Talk to me." She slipped an arm around Tracey's shoulders.

Molly had been with the family since Tracey was born, had served as her nanny as well as the housekeeper. Frank had been devastated when Tracey's mother died of a brain aneurysm, and it was Molly who had helped them get through the grieving process. She was short, slightly overweight, and had gray hair that she pulled up in a bun on top of her head. That day she wore a bright-red sweatshirt with Rudolph on the front and a pair of jeans.

"Daddy thinks maybe I've made myself sick because Austin hasn't called," Tracey answered.

"Maybe you have, but just to be sure you don't have something medically instead of heart-related wrong with you, I'm going to make you a doctor's appointment for tomorrow morning. I'm leaving on my vacation after supper tonight, but I expect you to call me as soon as you know something," Molly said.

"I will, and in case I forget, tell Gloria Ann hello for me," Tracey said.

"I will do that. She and the kids have been lookin' forward

to my trip down to Houston for weeks, but, honey, if this is something serious, I can turn right around and come back home." Molly patted her on the shoulder.

"It's nothing to worry about," Tracey assured her. "Just a bug that won't let go. I don't see any need in going to the doctor, but to make you feel better, I will."

"Good girl," Molly said. "Now go get some rest while I make supper. You'll feel better once you get some decent food in you."

The big house was as quiet as a tomb the next morning when Tracey went down to breakfast. She made herself a piece of toast and a cup of tea, sat alone at the table to nibble on it, and checked her phone a couple more times. Molly had managed to get her in to see their old family doctor at ten o'clock that morning. She had reminded Tracey the night before—as she walked out the door on her way to the airport—that it was his last appointment until after the new year.

Tracey felt a little better and thought maybe she might cancel the appointment. She was even scrolling down her contact list when a vision of her mother popped into her head. Laura had been a redhead with green eyes, and Tracey looked just like her. What if, like her mother, Tracey had something wrong in her head and this stomach issue was part of it? Better be safe than sorry—that's what her mother always told her.

She finished her breakfast, got dressed, drove across town to the medical complex, and was five minutes early to her appointment. Dr. Henson breezed into the room where the nurse had put her and said, "What's going on with you, Tracey? Molly said you've had a stomach problem."

Tracey told him about the shrimp she'd eaten on the ski trip and all the other symptoms she had had. "I did feel a little better this morning."

"First things first." Dr. Henson pulled a box from a drawer and pointed across the hall toward the restroom. "Let's be sure you're not pregnant before we start running tests."

Tracey shook her head slowly from side to side. "I can't be pregnant. I never miss a pill."

"Standard procedure," Dr. Henson said. "Just follow the directions and leave the stick on the counter. I'll be back in to talk to you in about ten minutes."

She did what she was supposed to and then went back to the room to wait. She had not missed a period, but the last two had been really light. Still, she couldn't be pregnant—no way—because she was faithful with her pills. She even set an alarm on her phone so she wouldn't forget to take one every day.

She paced the floor, back and forth from one end of the tiny examination room to the other and back again, then checked her phone. One minute had passed. Doc said he would be back in ten minutes, but the directions said the test would show positive or negative in sixty seconds. She opened the door and went back across the hallway, only to find the test was already gone. She dragged her heavy heart back to the room and looked at her phone. Two minutes had passed.

Her pulse raced when she heard the door open, and Dr. Henson came into the room. "Test is positive, which is a relief, girl. I'd rather you be pregnant than have a brain tumor. I'm going to refer you to a good ob-gyn in this complex. I'm going to take a guess and say you're probably about three to six weeks along since you're already experiencing morning sickness." He handed her a card. "You've got an appointment with Dr. Lenford on January 3. Your father has always wanted grandchildren. Tell him congratulations from me."

"Yes, sir." Tracey's mouth was so dry she could hardly speak as she took the card from the doctor's hands.

"Now go have a wonderful new year," the doctor said and disappeared out into the hallway.

She didn't even remember driving home, unlocking the

front door, or sinking down on the wingback chair beside the sideboard in the foyer. She was glad that her father and Molly were both gone for a few days. That gave her some time to think. Her phone rang, and for the first time in three weeks and one day, she hoped it wasn't Austin. She needed time to think about how to tell him this news. But as luck would have it, Austin's picture popped up on her screen. She laid the phone against her heart and took a deep breath. She could not answer it—not yet.

In a few minutes, it rang again, and she still couldn't make herself hit the accept icon. This time he left a message in her voicemail box.

"Trace, this is Austin. Call me, please. We need to talk really bad."

Get it over with. Her mother's voice was back in her head. *You'll fret and worry until you do.*

She scrolled down, hit the call button, and waited. Two rings, three, four.

Finally, Austin answered. "Hello, Trace." His voice sounded horrible, like maybe someone in his family had died.

She was making mental plans to go straight back to Durant when he said, "We've got to talk."

"Yes, we do. I've got something to tell you," she said.

"Me first," he said. "I'm getting married Friday night. I got drunk—"

Had he said *married*? Was she hearing things? The room spun around in circles, and the walls seemed to be closing in on her.

"What did you say?" she asked. "Is this a joke? If it is, it's not funny."

"It's not a joke." Austin's voice cracked. "There's no easy way to explain this. The night I got home—after we had that hellacious argument—a couple of friends treated me to a few beers. And the beers turned into boilermakers."

He paused.

"Okay. You went on a bender. So?"

"Well, I didn't go on a bender all by myself."

"You were with friends."

"One of them was a female friend."

"I see, and what does that have to do with you getting married?" Tears streamed down her cheeks and dripped onto her jacket.

"I wound up in bed with Crystal Smith," Austin said.

"Why?" That was the only word she could get out.

"She was there, and I was mad at you," he said.

"Who's Crystal Smith?"

"Just a girl from over around Luella, the next town over. You don't know her. She worked in the bar where we were having drinks," he explained. "She's pregnant. That's why I'm marryin' her. There isn't any other option. You know how I feel about stuff like that. And no child of mine is ever goin' to wonder who his daddy is."

Tears continued to roll down Tracey's cheeks.

"I see," she said.

"Is that all you've got to say?" he said.

"How about goodbye?"

"Don't let it end this way, Tracey. I still love you, and always will, but she's carrying my baby. She's been sick for a couple of days, and she went to the doctor today. She's only three weeks, which is the right timing."

"Don't say that you love me! Don't you dare!" Tracey groaned.

"This woman is carryin' my baby. I got to do what's right. I'll have to quit college and just take online courses to finish up my degree, so I won't even see you in Durant. I just had to explain…"

"Goodbye, Austin," she whispered as she ended the call. Then she dropped the phone on the floor and sobbed while her heart shattered into a million pieces, the jagged edges cutting apart her soul.

Chapter 3

TRACEY PROPPED HER SCHEDULE UP ON THE STEERING WHEEL of her old Camaro and drove slowly, glancing down at the paper at every stoplight to get the day's events in her mind. Eight thirty. Faculty get-acquainted breakfast. Stale doughnuts and watery coffee, she would guess, and lots of names to remember. Some kindly gray-haired professor who'd been at Southeastern since the magnolia trees were saplings would lead her around like a prize puppy dog. She would be introduced to people who probably wouldn't remember *her* name by lunchtime.

She nosed the car into a vacant spot in the faculty parking lot, picked up her briefcase and the piece of paper that told her what to do and when to do it all day, and started across the campus. Last month, when she had accepted a job in the

English Department, was the first time she'd been back to Southeastern Oklahoma State University in almost six years.

Not much had changed. The twin tower dorm still rose up at the north side of the campus, the big magnolia trees still shaded the lawns, the sidewalks still had the same cracks, and the fountain in the middle of the campus still waited for the freshmen students to dump in a bottle of extra-sudsy dish detergent for its yearly bubble bath.

It was a bit scary to come back to Durant after all these years—even scarier to return to Southeastern as a teacher instead of a student—but they'd made her a good offer where she could work on her doctorate, and now she would be among the youngest professors at the university.

A student passed her in front of the library. He wore a T-shirt, tight blue jeans, and cowboy boots that were down at the heels. His long legs and easy stride reminded her of Austin, but she shook the memory from her mind. She had vowed when she'd accepted this job not to dwell on the past.

Austin probably lived in some backwater town in Texas now. She wondered if he'd gotten the degree he'd been so determined to have. Or had he just given up and gone into emu ranching or some other damn silly enterprise?

Stop it, she scolded herself. *Austin was a good man. We*

both made bad choices. If I'd called him that night and asked to work things out, things could have turned out different. But I didn't and all choices have consequences.

She went to the ladies' room for one more mirror check before she pasted on a smile and tried to dust off her system for remembering names. She dabbed sweat from her forehead, freshened her makeup, and tightened the wide, soft leather belt that cinched in her beige linen sleeveless dress. August was always hot in southern Oklahoma, and just walking across the lawn had caused her to break a sweat.

Maybe she shouldn't have worn something sleeveless for her first day back. Maybe the chic dress was too revealing for the new Comp I teacher. Oh well, it was too late now to think about that. At least it was long enough, ending just a few inches from her ankles where the straps from her kid leather sandals made several wraps before tying into perfect little bows.

She checked her watch. It was eight thirty on the dot. She couldn't procrastinate any longer. She only hoped that she could remember some of the people and wouldn't make too many mistakes later on when she ran into the professors and teachers on campus.

"Hello." She approached the student behind the desk

outside the double doors leading into the ballroom. "I'm Tracey Walker."

"Okay." The girl smiled. "Let's see, there's a name tag here somewhere. Did you say Tracey or Stacey?"

"Tracey."

"Oh, here it is. This your first year here?" the girl asked.

"My first year as a teacher. I went to school at Southeastern several years ago." She smiled back at the girl. "Am I late?"

"No, but I'm supposed to notify Dr. Taylor when you get here so she can introduce you to everyone. She's head of the English Department. Been here forever, I hear. Personally, I think she just squatted out here in a pasture one day and they built the school around her." The girl's southern Oklahoma drawl even came through in her giggle.

Tracey chuckled. She remembered Dr. Taylor well. She had always been forming committees and starting organizations to promote one worthy cause or another. Tracey had admired her energy and enthusiasm even back then.

"Well, I don't want to disappoint the lady. Tell her I'm here and ready to be introduced." Tracey pulled the back off the self-adhesive name tag and slapped it on her dress right above her heart.

"There you are. You must be our brand-new Comp I

teacher." A short, overweight lady bustled toward her with her hand stuck out. "I'm Dr. Taylor and… Oh dear, I forgot, I've got to make a presentation in a few minutes. Do you think you could show Miss Walker around, Becky? I think most everyone is here, and if you'll lay out the name tags, the latecomers can just pick them up."

"Sure thing, Dr. Taylor." Becky motioned for Tracey to follow her. "Like I said, she's always busy. I'm Becky Green, and I'm a sophomore here at Southeastern. I'm enrolled in your Comp I class this semester. I should have taken it last year, but I had a scheduling conflict," she said as she led the way into the ballroom. "Care for some coffee? I wondered how Dr. Taylor was going to introduce you to everyone here in just fifteen minutes."

"Looks like you've got the job now, and I'd love a cup of coffee," Tracey answered. "You seem to know your way around. What's your major, or have you chosen one?"

"Criminal justice. Daddy says I watch too many cop shows, but all that stuff intrigues me." Becky was a pretty girl, shorter than Tracey by several inches, and slim. She wore a denim skirt, red lace-up Roper boots, and a sleeveless white shirt decorated across the front with silver conchos held on with strips of red leather. A few freckles decorated her turned-up nose, and her brown eyes didn't stray from the bathroom door.

"You're not from Oklahoma, are you?" Tracey asked.

Becky shook her head, made her way over to the coffee table, and returned with a steaming cup. She handed it off to Tracey and said, "I'm from southern Louisiana. About as far as you can go without falling into the Gulf of Mexico. Little town called Cameron."

"How little?" Tracey asked.

"My graduating class had nineteen in it, and I'm one of five who went on to college," Becky said.

"What did you find different from your part of the world and this one?" Tracey asked.

"I miss rice." Becky smiled. "Folks up here eat potatoes and more beef. We have more fish and rice, and I was used to the Gulf, where I could see all the way from beach to horizon. This little Red River is just a fishing hole to us, and it don't even have crawdads," she answered in a sweet southern voice.

Red River deep. Tracey shut her eyes and willed the memory to fade.

"You okay? You look a little like you just saw a ghost. Forgot to ask if you wanted sugar or cream."

"I'm fine," Tracey lied. "I take it black, thanks."

She sipped the coffee without even tasting it, until a tall, blond-haired man edged through the crowd and stood right in front of her. Tracey took a deep breath and prepared herself mentally to meet and greet. The man spoke first. "Hey, let me introduce myself. I'm Damian Marshall from the Chemistry Department. I haven't seen you before." His eyes started at the toes of her sandals and traveled up slowly past her curvy hips, her belted waist, stopping for a moment at the name tag, and then went on to the top of her head where the ends of her long, red hair ruffled out in curls at the finish of a French twist.

Just that much put Tracey on instant alert and creeped her out.

He slowly dropped his gaze back down to her eyes and stuck out his hand.

"This is Tracey Walker." Becky's voice dripped with ice as she made introductions. "She's the new English Comp I teacher."

"Pleased to meet you." Tracey shook his hand "Damian Marshall, is it?" She applied her word association. Damian... devil. He looked like a devil with those black eyes.

Becky pulled on her arm. "Miz Walker, I want to introduce you to Dr. Benson. He's my favorite American Lit professor."

Tracey barely had time to excuse herself from Devil—no, Damian! She'd remember his name if she tried hard enough.

"Stay away from him," Becky whispered when they were out of earshot. "He tries to get every new teacher and every new student to drop her underwear for him. Thinks he's God's gift to womankind. Don't ever get caught in a building at night with him. Not even the library."

"Is this the voice of experience I'm hearing?" Tracey asked.

"Yes, ma'am. I had a run-in with him the first week I was here. In the library elevator. I thought I was goin' to have to knock him in the head with my lit book. I never knew one man could have so many hands and try to 'accidentally'"— she put quotes around the last word—"put them in so many places. Now I check the elevators before I get on them."

"That's sexual harassment," Tracey said.

"Yep, it is, and I'm not the only one who's complained, but he's got some kind of connections around here because no one listens to us." She stopped and said, "Dr. Benson, I want you to meet Tracey Walker, our new Comp I teacher."

Tracey turned and found herself in front of a tall, lanky professor who sported more wrinkles on his face than there were lines on an Oklahoma road map. His blue eyes were lively, and he immediately stuck out his hand.

"So glad to meet you, Miz Walker," he said. "We met briefly when you came to interview for the job. I'm glad you decided to join us."

"Thank you, Dr. Benson. I'm glad to be here," Tracey said as she shook hands with him. "I remember meeting you at that interview."

"Just Matt to the faculty," he said.

"That's all right. How long have you been at Southeastern?" Tracey asked. "I was a student here about six years ago and I don't remember you from then."

"Just five years. I was teaching at Baylor in Waco, Texas, and decided I needed a change of scenery and a smaller campus." Someone tapped him on the shoulder, and he turned, losing himself in another group before Tracey could answer.

Becky tugged on her arm again. "Oh, there's my other favorite teacher. You've just got to come and meet him."

"How many favorite teachers do you have?" Tracey followed her through the small groups of people toward the far side of the room.

"Dr. Benson is my most favorite." Becky stopped. "He's the nicest person in the whole school system. Lord, if I had the chicken pox, I wouldn't even care if he came to see me in my black-and-white cow pajamas and Donald Duck house shoes.

He's a sweetheart and we all adore him. There's not a girl on campus who wouldn't lie down on a six-lane highway and die happy if he would just smile at her once." She sighed.

"Holy smoke. I didn't know movie stars taught school down here in southern Oklahoma." Tracey laughed out loud.

"Huh!" Becky snorted. "There isn't a movie star's smile that compares to his. And the way he looks in jeans…" She let out a long sigh. "It's just not fair that there's a rule about professors and students dating. I mean, after all he's only six or seven years older than I am."

"Do you think I should go check my lipstick? Are there crumbs on my dress? Do I have a coffee mustache?" Tracey teased.

"You look wonderful. He'll like you, especially with your red hair. He's got a little redheaded daughter he just dotes on." Becky started walking again. "Damn. He just went in the restroom. We'll have to wait."

"A daughter? Where's his wife?" Tracey asked.

Becky's long, straight brown hair swirled around her shoulders when she shook her head. "He doesn't have one."

Tracey turned around to set her empty cup on one of the long folding tables set up with chairs around them and wondered about this amazing man with a daughter and no wife.

"He's out now," Becky said. "You asked about his wife. There's all kinds of rumors. He got married and she left him for some reason and he's raisin' the little girl all alone. She's a cute little thing and so smart it's scary. When he brings her to the campus, we all fight over who gets to play with her." Becky talked as she led the way across the room.

Several men had their backs to them as they crossed the room, all of them facing Dr. Benson, who was gesturing with his hands as he told a story. When the professor noticed the two women walking toward his group, he beckoned them over.

"Come on over here and meet some more of the faculty. I've forgotten your name already." He chuckled. "Maybe my wife is right. Maybe I am getting senile. I can't even remember someone as beautiful as you are," he teased. When he said *beautiful*, all four men turned around to look at her.

Tracey focused on the first man on her right. He was short, balding, and wearing dark-blue slacks, with a light-blue dress shirt and black loafers. "This is David Robbins. He's our librarian," Dr. Benson said. Tracey looked at him long enough to get his name in her mind, then turned to the next man. He was taller and had a little more hair. "This is Lance Mendoza. He teaches Spanish." Dr. Benson smiled. The third man had lots of red hair and a roll of fat around his middle. "And this feller is Earl Tramble. We play a little golf together when he can get out of the Biology Department, and this last feller here is—"

A chill chased down Tracey's spine as she looked up into Austin Miller's blue eyes.

"Hello, Trace, it's been a long time," Austin said. "I saw your name on the new faculty staff list. Welcome back to Durant."

She was completely speechless, but her mind was spinning with questions. Austin was a professor? How did that happen? He'd told her he was quitting college. No, that's not right. He'd mentioned doing online courses.

"Oh, do you two already know each other?" Becky's eyes darted back and forth between them. "Imagine that."

"Yes, we know each other. We were in school here at the same time," Austin drawled, and his eyes never left Tracey's. "But that was a while ago."

"Well, you two need to catch up, then," Dr. Benson said. "You'll have lots of time to do that since you have offices on the same floor of your building. Small world, isn't it?"

"Yes, sir, it surely is," Austin answered without turning away from Tracey.

He was even sexier, if that was possible, than he'd been back when they were both twenty years old.

"It's good to see you again," Tracey finally said even though she was breathless. "It has been a long time."

"Yes, it has," Austin said. "A little more than six and a half years, if I remember right."

Becky touched Tracey on the arm. "Don't forget. You've got an English Department meeting at nine thirty. We should be going."

"I suppose I'll see you around," Tracey said to Austin.

"I'll be at the nine-thirty meeting. I'm working as an adjunct while I work on my doctorate." He waved and turned back to listen to Dr. Benson.

"I think I do need to make a quick trip to the ladies' room," Tracey whispered to Becky. "I'll just be a minute. Meet you by the coffee urn when I get out?"

"Sure," Becky said.

Tracey shut the bathroom door and leaned against it, wishing she could slide down it and plop onto the floor. She was afraid if she did, her jelly-filled knees would never support her again. Would it be possible for her to get out of the contract she'd signed so easily just last month? Could the English Department find another teacher with only three days left until classes started?

She stared at her reflection in the mirror. "Get it together, woman! You can't stay in the bathroom all day. You are strong. You are smart, and you will be professional."

She had to go outside and pretend she'd barely known Austin all those years ago. She couldn't let Becky know she'd loved him deeply, and that at one time they'd talked of marriage. "God, why didn't I think to check the faculty list?" she groaned as she washed her hands and dried them on a brown paper towel.

Austin was supposed to be off somewhere with his poor little wife, living in a broken-down trailer house without a porch. Finally, she pushed out of the bathroom and found Becky, who was waiting patiently by the coffee urn.

"I thought I was going to introduce you to the handsomest man I'd ever seen and you already knew him," she said. "Tell me, was he as good-looking when he was young? Or did he have pimples and a weird haircut? Was he a real dork that turned into a hunk?"

"No, not that I remember," Tracey mumbled. "It's about time for me to get to the next meeting. Becky, you've been a big help this morning. Come by my office and see me anytime. Let's go out to lunch someday. My treat. Thanks for showing me around and all the inside information about Devil...I mean, Damian."

Becky laughed. "That's a good name for that bastard. Devil Damian. You know, I bet he wears his hair that way to cover up the horns." She got a case of the giggles that ended in hiccups. "I'd better go get a drink of water. I'll come by next week and take you up on that lunch offer." She headed toward the fountain in the hallway, still giggling.

Tracey picked up her briefcase and checked her watch. She simply could not go into the meeting with stars in her eyes and any idea she could pick up where she left off with Austin six years ago. Granted, he didn't have a wife, but he did have a daughter, and she had a son that was now the love of her life.

Jackson had been her salvation in a world of heartache and pain.

She would have to be careful and keep her private life and her business life entirely separate. She'd be the best damned Comp I teacher this university had ever hired, but the day her contract ran out, she'd have everything in the apartment packed and ready to move. It didn't matter where. Just so long as Austin Miller wasn't where she was going.

She found a bench beside the fountain and sat down under the magnolia trees. It was already hot. *Oklahoma in August really is seven times hotter than hell*, she thought. Her daddy had always said that and had added that it was a wonder the churches didn't have a list of folks ready, willing, and waiting to make sure they had their reservations in heaven secured. Tiny rivulets of sweat ran down her cleavage and soaked the elastic band at the bottom of her bra. Wonderful. She probably had underarm circles on her linen dress, too.

Tracey hoped Austin was as uncomfortable as she was. She hoped his glands were working overtime and he was being smothered by those starched Wrangler jeans with the sharp creases, and that white shirt with finely ironed lines down the sleeves. It was a cinch he had had them done at the laundry. There wasn't a man alive who could iron that well. His jeans were bunched up at the bottom around the tops of freshly polished black Roper boots, and he had on a silver belt buckle with a bronco on it. He sure didn't look like a university English professor, and he damned sure didn't look like a drugstore cowboy. He looked like the real thing.

No more thinking about Austin, she fussed at herself. *You're over him. He's not going to be part of your new life. You've worked hard for what you have. You got your bachelor's and your master's degree and doctorate while you raised Jackson. And you've done it on your own without any help from anyone. So you can control your thoughts and your emotions.*

With that self-inflicted lecture over, she stood up, straightened her back, held her chin high, and proceeded toward the classroom building for the department meeting. She thought of Jackson, her little boy. His ready smile, his honesty, his undivided and undying love for her. She would think of him when she was in the room with Austin and know beyond any doubt that she could walk this balance beam for one year without falling off.

Tracey picked up a pocket folder with her name on it from the table at the front of the room when she arrived. On the far side of the room was a table full of teachers with only one chair left, and she sat down and introduced herself to the others. She spotted Austin sitting at a table on the other side of the room and willed herself to smile and wave.

"Now." Dr. Taylor tapped on the table in front of her with a pencil. "Each of you has a folder with your name on it. It outlines what the objectives are in your field and the goals we hope to accomplish by the end of this year. In Comp I we want to be able to track positive progress in writing ability. We want to see the student able to write a simple sentence, a complex sentence, a compound-complex sentence, and a complete paper utilizing every one of these…"

Tracey rifled through the pages in her folder. Not too

different from the objectives and outlooks the state mandated for high school teachers. Nothing she couldn't handle for the year ahead. She reminded herself again that she had been hired for only one year. After that, she and Jackson could wave goodbye to Durant, Oklahoma, as they watched it fade in the rearview mirror of her old red Camaro.

Chapter 4

THE FIRST WEEK OF SCHOOL WAS SO BUSY THAT TRACEY didn't know straight up from due backwards. She saw Austin a few times in the hallway either heading in the direction of their adjoining offices or else in a rush toward the steps. Dashing down the stairs and off to the next class or appointment was certainly preferable to waiting for the slow elevator to groan its way up and down.

By the time her head hit the pillow at night, her eyes were already closed, and her mind was already shutting down with no thoughts of the past, present, or future, only a sigh of gratefulness for a few hours of rest. The last thing that went through her mind, just before she fell asleep, was a guilty feeling for not spending more time with Jackson. She promised herself wearily that tomorrow she would put everything else on the back burner and spend a whole hour with him. They'd talk about whatever he wanted to, do what he wanted, take a long walk, take a swim in the swimming pool at the apartment complex—the same place that she'd lived in before, only this time she couldn't get one on the ground floor. However, they did have an elevator and Jackson loved pushing the button to go up to their second-floor "partyment" as he called it. And he adored the balcony where he pretended that he was the king and the whole complex was his castle.

By the end of the second week, things began to become more routine. A few students still dropped classes occasionally, but for the most part everyone seemed to have settled into the way things were going to be for the rest of the semester. The administration office had assigned Twyla to her as a student aide two hours a day. The young lady was a data processor who could make the computer do anything but sit up and tell jokes. She had a phone voice that sounded like sweet cream, and she kept the files wonderfully organized.

That morning Tracey dropped Jackson off at kindergarten, and since the traffic wasn't horrible, she got to her office a few minutes early. "Got anything important?" she asked as she dropped a stack of papers on the filing cabinet with a thud and melted into the swivel chair behind her desk.

"No, just a couple of calls from the textbook publisher on your memo pad there." Twyla motioned with her hand.

She was as tall as Tracey and a lot thinner, but then Twyla was a basketball player who got a hard workout every day in the gym. Give her ten years, and she might add twenty pounds just as Tracey had. Her brown hair was parted in the middle and hung to her shoulders. Her nose was slightly too long and had a funny little hump right in the middle, but her smile showed off beautiful, even white teeth.

"Okay," Tracey said. "I'll call them back. By the way, thanks for all your hard work. You're making my first semester of teaching a lot easier."

"That's what I'm here for." Twyla checked her watch. "Gotta run. My biology class starts in five minutes." She waved as she left the room.

"Thank God it's Friday," Tracey muttered as she removed a bottle of water from the refrigerator beside her desk. "Three classes of Comp I today, and then I get to go home to my son at noon."

She carried her water down the hall and into her first class of the day. "Good morning," she said. "We've discussed and written a sentence and a paragraph. As you all know if you've looked at your syllabus, your next assignment, due on

Monday, is a five-hundred-word essay on what you expected when you started college and how it's different from the reality you have found."

There were a few groans and lots of long sighs from the students.

"I'll expect to see my inbox flooded no later than Monday night at midnight. Anything that comes in after that will automatically drop one letter grade. Any assignment that is two days late becomes an automatic zero. Now let's go over sentence structure and paragraph development one more time," she said.

Tracey finished the last class for the day at eleven o'clock and had started back to her office to get her briefcase before she headed home. She would have plenty of time to stop by the grocery store and maybe one of those rentals outside the Dollar General to get that new Disney movie for Jackson. Then she intended to take off her professor hat, put on her mommy hat, and enjoy the whole weekend. She slipped her laptop into her briefcase and locked her office door behind her as she left.

She heard the elevator doors open and rushed to get inside before they closed again.

"Which floor?" a familiar voice asked.

She turned around and was face-to-face in a small, enclosed space with Derrick—no, that wasn't right. *Think, Tracey*, she thought. *His name isn't Derrick. It's Devil. No, Damian. That's it.*

"First floor, and thank you," she answered without looking at him.

He pushed the button and brushed past her, and when the elevator started down with a jerk, he fell right into her. One hand landed on her breast, and the other around her shoulders.

"Sorry about that," he said as he took a step back, but his smile told her that he did it on purpose. "I think you tripped me."

"No, sir, I did not, and you don't fool me one bit with your sly moves." She hoped her tone was cold enough to put him off.

"No moves here, honey." He grinned and dragged out the last word into several syllables. "You can make it up to me by going out to dinner with me tonight."

"No, thanks. I have plans." She took a step toward the doors to be ready as soon as they opened.

He lowered his voice to a whisper. "It's Friday night. The whole weekend is ahead of us. It's just dinner. You have to eat."

"I said no," she said.

"A rain check then," he persisted.

"Probably not," she said as the elevator doors opened.

Becky was right there, but when she saw Damian, her smile faded, and she took a step back. "Hey, you are just the person I wanted to see, Miz Walker. Would it be all right if I walk out with you? I want to ask a couple of questions before I start writing that paper that's due on Monday."

"Sure thing." Tracey smiled.

"Thanks a bunch," Becky said.

"Thank *you*," Tracey said when they were out of the building. "He really is creepy."

"Oh yeah, and I lied," Becky said. "I've already finished my assignment. I just have to go over it again and then I'll send it to you. I worked ahead from the syllabus that you gave us. A bunch of us are going to the Silver Spur tonight to do some line dancing. I didn't want to try to write with a hangover. I was really going up to the second floor to wait on a friend, but I didn't want to get into the elevator with old Devil Dog. So it's me that should be thanking you."

Tracey nodded. "I wish any of you girls he harasses would go straight to the dean with it."

"We have, and Damian says that we're making a mountain out of a molehill," Becky said.

Tracey said, "That's what he says, but if every one of you

protests to the dean when he harasses you, pretty soon someone will pay attention. Promise me that you will."

"I promise. Thanks, Mom," Becky threw over her shoulder as she jogged across the quad toward the parking lot.

"I'm not your mom!" Tracey called after her as she headed
in the opposite direction.

She got into her car, closed the door, and started the
engine. The AC was still on from her morning drive in, so the
car began to cool off immediately. Tracey laid her head on the
steering wheel and closed her eyes. Sure, she'd shown Damian
who was in control, but she felt dirty all the same. She ripped
a tissue from the box on the floor behind the passenger seat
and rubbed her neck with it. To think he'd actually touched
her made her skin crawl.

There was no one to talk to, to tell how horrible he made
her feel. She certainly couldn't tell her Jackson about it, and
she had to be brave in front of Becky. She envied girls and
women with mothers who were still alive. This was a time
to call a mother and listen to her say, "You poor baby. Next
time he does something like that, kill the dirty bastard, and
I'll help you bury his sorry body." But her mother had been
dead since she was thirteen.

The passenger door opened, and Tracey jumped as if she

had just been touched with a cattle prod. Every raw nerve in her body was ready to go to battle.

"Are you all right?" Austin asked.

"I'm fine," she said. "Just tired from a long week."

"I don't believe you." He slid into the passenger's seat. "This hasn't gotten a bit bigger since the last time I rode in this car. I'm surprised that you haven't traded it in for something newer and flashier."

"It still runs, and it's paid for," Tracey said. "And I'm fine, but I had a run-in with Damian in the elevator."

"Did he hurt you?" Austin looked genuinely worried. "Tell me honestly, Trace, did he?"

"No, he just invited me to dinner, but..." She paused. "How did a man like that ever get a job here?"

"He's got connections with some folks who have power," Austin answered. "One of these days, he's going to cross over the line with the wrong person."

"I hope so," Tracey said. "You need a ride somewhere?"

"No, I'm parked right behind you. I just saw you here with your head on the steering wheel and thought you might be sick. I should be going now," he said.

"Thanks for worrying about me, but I can take care of myself," she said.

"I have no doubt about that, but we really need to talk. It's been too long since we did."

"Maybe someday, but not today. I've got errands to run. And, Austin, we said our goodbyes a long time ago. You went your way, and I've gone mine. We're different people now. We're not those two lovestruck kids that we were back then!"

"We all make mistakes," Austin said. "God knows I've made enough for two men. If you ever want to talk, let me know." He got out of the car and walked back to a fairly new black pickup truck.

Her heart pounded and her pulse raced as she watched him in the rearview mirror. She had really thought she was over him, but evidently out of sight didn't work with Austin.

More like absence makes the heart grow fonder. Her father's voice popped into her head.

"You're right, Daddy," she whispered, "but I'll get over him."

She backed the car out and made a couple of turns until she was on University Boulevard and headed west. At the red light, she made another right toward the elementary school where Jackson was in kindergarten.

By the time she parked the car and walked up the sidewalk,

children were pouring out of the building. Jackson came running as fast as his little legs would carry him.

"Mommy, wait till you see what we made in arts and crafts today. It's a butterfly! You can put it on our refrigerator door beside the dinosaur I made a long time ago. I'm hungry. Can we go get an ice cream?" He jumped into her outstretched arms.

"How about we change our plans and go to McDonald's for burgers and ice cream, then we'll play in the park and go to the movies." She nuzzled her face into his neck, breathing in the scent of a sweaty little boy and thinking it was the most wonderful smell in the whole world.

"You mean it? Whoopee! This town must be bigger'n you said it was if it's got a McDonald's *and* a movie theater. Wow!"

She set him down but continued to hold on to his hand while they walked across the street together to the car. "Does the park have swings, Mommy?" he asked.

"Yes, it does," she said, giggling. "And a big slide. And it's got a kid-size merry-go-round, but I'm not getting on it. You know how sick it makes me to go 'round and 'round."

"Girls aren't tough as us guys. I bet a boy could stay on the merry-go-round for three days and not get sick," Jackson declared as he crawled into the back seat of the car and buckled his seat belt. "Time for takeoff now." He used his pencil for a microphone and pretended he was the pilot of a plane. "Fasten your seat belts, ladies and gentlemen. We're flying with a lady pilot and she's hell on wheels."

"Jackson! Where did you hear that word!" she scolded.

"Poppa Frank says it all the time. He says you were hell on wheels from the first time you drove," Jackson said, all wide-eyed with innocence.

"Well, Poppa Frank can say that word if he wants to, but you're not to repeat what he says." She bit back a smile. "Now tell me all about your day," she said. "Did you color and play or what did you do?"

"I learned," he said. "I learned all about everything, and I made a new best friend. She's a girl, and she's just as much fun as the boys."

"Glad to hear it. What's your new best friend's name?" Tracey asked as she drove toward McDonald's on the west side of town.

"Her name is Emily. I wanted to bring her to meet you. She's got red hair like yours and she's really nice for a girl. But her daddy already came and got her 'afore you got there. She's going to see her granny this weekend. Her granny lives in a place with a funny name. Pork 'n' Beans, Texas, or something like that."

"What's her last name?" Tracey wanted to lay her head on the steering wheel again, but she just took a deep breath and crossed her fingers that the little red-haired girl wasn't Austin's daughter.

"Emily Miller," Jackson said. "And I think she's going to Tom Bean, Texas. That's a funny name for a town, isn't it, Mama? How far is it to Texas anyway? Maybe we could go down there and see her and her granny sometime. She said if I would come to her granny's house, I could pet her pony. How far is it to McDonald's? I'm real hungry."

Chapter 5

Somehow by good luck, good timing, or the good grace of the Almighty, Tracey managed to pick her son up at school for the next two weeks without running into Austin. Since that awful day when Damian had accosted her and Austin had said they needed to talk, she had been able to avoid him.

If she could continue to keep Austin at a distance, she just might make it through this year, she thought as she and Jackson loaded up that Friday afternoon to drive north to see her father. Jackson loved his Poppa Frank, and Tracey had to admit he was a better grandfather than she'd ever expected, especially considering the circumstances.

Frank Walker hadn't been around much when Tracey was growing up, and her mother had been on the road a lot with her business. Their housekeeper, Molly, had been the one to hold Tracey and tell her bedtime stories, teach her bedtime prayers and table manners, and tell her about boys when that time came. Then her mother had died when Tracey was only thirteen and her father had never quite gotten it through his stubborn head that Tracey wasn't a little girl anymore.

Jackson played with his video game in the back seat, and Tracey let her mind wander back to when she couldn't hide her pregnancy anymore. Molly was the first to finally notice the baby bump and informed her that she had a choice— she could tell her father that she was pregnant that night at supper or Molly would.

"Daddy, I'm pregnant," she had blurted out the moment they sat down to the table. She didn't know if he would kick her out of the house or cry in disappointment. She'd only seen Frank Walker cry one time in her life—and that was at her mother's funeral.

"How far along are you?" he had asked.

"Six months," she had whispered. "That's why I wanted to stay home and do online courses this past semester."

"Who's the father?" Frank hadn't shed tears, but he looked so disappointed in her that she began to weep.

She had shaken her head. "It doesn't matter who he is. This is my mistake and my baby."

"Is it Austin Miller's?" Frank had asked. "That was your last boyfriend, the one who wouldn't meet me, or did you have a one-night stand when you went on that skiing trip?"

"I'm not saying," Tracey said.

"What do you intend to do about it?" her dad had asked.

"I'm going to have the baby and raise him. It's a boy. I had an ultrasound." She remembered she hadn't been able to talk above a whisper as she got it all out. "I applied for a job at Oklahoma City University in the library, and I'm going to do some online tutoring. I've rented an apartment close to the school, and I'm going to be moving up there next week."

"That's not necessary." Frank's voice was as clear in her head as it had been back then.

"Mama, how many more miles is it?" Jackson asked. "I can't wait to see Poppa Frank and tell him all about my new friend, Emily. She can even ride a horse. Do you think I'll ever get to ride a horse, Mama? I really want to, but I'm just a little bit afraid. Horses are so big that they kinda scare me, but don't tell Emily. I don't want her to think I'm a sissy. She can't swim, though, and I can swim. We've got a pool at our apartment place. Why don't we ever go swimmin'?" Jackson asked.

Daddy, did I ever ask this many questions? Tracey wondered.

"We will go swimming next week, I promise, and someday maybe you can learn to ride horses, and I bet Emily wouldn't think you were a sissy." She hoped that answered all his questions.

"Mama, you said that you named me after Poppa Frank, but who is Nelson?" Jackson asked. "You never told me that. Emily has only got one grandpa, too, but some of the kids in my room at school have two grandpas. Why does me and Emily only have one?"

"That's a story for another day." Tracey was more than glad to see the exit for Purcell.

What are you going to tell him when he asks if this is the day that you tell him why he's only got one grandpa? Sometimes Tracey wished that her father wouldn't pop into her head.

"I'll cross that bridge when I get to it," she whispered.

Are you going to tell him the same thing you told me about where his name came from?

Tracey smiled at the memory of what she'd told her father when he'd asked the same question.

"From a love story I read once," she had said back then and let her father think that the name came from a romance book.

"Your name came from a person I knew a long time ago," she answered her son. "And you only have one grandpa because you are special."

Neither of those answers was a lie. Jackson was special, and she had known Austin a long time ago.

━━━━━━━━

The weekend passed by too quickly, and Jackson was so tired that he slept the whole way home to Durant. Days went by slowly that week, or so it seemed, but on Friday, Tracey wondered where the time had gone. As soon as her last class was over, she rushed from the college to the First Day of Fall play that Jackson's class was presenting. He had practiced his songs until he could sing them without a hitch, and he'd been chosen to lead the class by reciting the first line in a funny poem. He knew it so well that he delivered it with a theatrical flair, using exaggerated gestures that made her laugh.

This was the first school event that she and Austin would be attending, and she sent up a silent prayer on the drive from the university to the elementary school that their paths wouldn't cross. Austin would be there to see his daughter, she was sure, but if she sat at the back of the auditorium, she could slip down the aisle, gather Jackson up, and go out the back door just as soon as the play was done.

The auditorium was dark and cool, but Tracey could see the children all lined up in the front rows. She could feel the energy in the air and felt sorry for the teachers who were trying to maintain some semblance of control over all the kids. Austin came in, walked right past her, and sat down about three rows up from her. She felt as if her prayer had been answered.

The already dim lights went completely out, and Tracey could hear the shuffle of little feet marching up the steps to the stage. Then the curtains parted in the middle and Jackson stepped out. "Ladies and gentlemen," he shouted. "Welcome to our First Day of Fall play. We'll sing and say poems and you can clap and have a good time." Then he disappeared behind the curtains.

They sang a song about a worm in an apple and another one about a playmate coming out to holler down a rain barrel and slide down a cellar door, and then there was one about leaves falling, and after that a poem about football weather. Jackson hadn't even known what a rain barrel was or a cellar door, but he'd asked a million questions while he was learning the song. A little red-haired girl stood right beside him most of the time. Tracey wondered if that was Emily, Austin's daughter.

The program lasted exactly thirty minutes, and then the curtains parted slightly for the second time. Jackson and Emily stepped out from behind them together.

"Thank you for coming to our program," she said, loud and clear.

"And now for the surprise," Jackson added. "We're having a tea party in our classroom for all you folks who clapped for us."

Forget about sneaking out the back door. Tracey knew Jackson would definitely want her to meet his new best friend, so that meant Austin would be close at hand.

Once they were in the cafeteria where the tea party was held, she spotted Austin right away, standing in the corner surrounded by women.

Probably divorceés taking turns at trying out for his woman of the week, she thought.

Maybe they'd keep him busy until she could swallow a cup of lukewarm punch, eat a cookie, and entice Jackson away by reminding him that they were going to see Poppa Frank again that weekend.

"Oh, Mrs. Miller!" a short lady yelled across the room.

The room went so quiet that Tracey figured they could hear—not just see—her blushing as the woman pointed right at her.

"Mrs. Miller, over here!" The woman waved and smiled.

Tracey hoped that there was a woman standing somewhere near her that the lady was talking to, but no such luck.

"Emily, come here, darling, and introduce me to your mother," the woman said.

Tracey let out a long sigh of relief and wondered why Austin hadn't told anyone that he had remarried.

"My mama isn't here, but my daddy is." Emily's red curls bobbed up and down and the full skirt of her dress flipped from one side to the other as the child ran across the room.

"We talked about you and Jackson playing jokes on me." The woman kept walking straight toward Tracey until she was close enough to stick out her hand. "I'm Lori Baker, the new teacher's aide. I'm so glad you came to the program. I just wanted you to know that I think Emily is a sweetheart. She and Jackson have quite a sense of humor. They're always playing jokes on me, but not today. That child looks just like you."

"This isn't my mother. That's Jackson's mommy." Emily giggled. "That's my daddy over there, though."

"Oh, I'm so sorry." Lori flushed. "It's just that you have such lovely hair and Emily's is the same color...and...I'm just so sorry."

"Quite all right," Tracey muttered and started for the door, hoping to corner Jackson and get out while everyone was chuckling about the mix-up.

"She's not Emily's mommy," Jackson shouted from across the room. "She's mine," he said possessively.

Tracey wished for a hole to crawl into, one just big enough for her and her son to curl up inside and pull the opening in behind them.

"Mommy!" he shouted again and ran through the crowd to her side. "This is Emily, my bestest friend in the whole world. She does look like you, doesn't she? Emily, this is my mommy." He grabbed his little friend's hand. "Let's go get another cookie, Emily. Mommy, don't go away. You'll stay right here, won't you?"

"Yes, Jackson, I'll be right here." She sighed.

Tracey had no doubts that Austin would be asking about Jackson as soon as he could make his way to her side. Those women surrounding him couldn't begin to know how much she would pay them to keep him hemmed in for just ten minutes. She'd sell her Camaro and consider hocking her iPad if they'd hold him down five more minutes so she could get out of town for three days and collect her thoughts.

He must have said his goodbyes to his fan club because he began to edge his way through several other small groups toward her. She watched him out of the corner of her eye and proceeded to make her way to the door at the same speed. If he moved past one group, she moved to another, introducing herself and making small talk about how cute the play had been.

"Daddy!" Emily stood in the middle of the room and scanned it.

When Austin held up a hand, she flashed an angelic smile and ran over to him, grabbed his hand, and dragged him to the refreshment stand.

"Come see Jackson," she said. "He's my new friend I told you about."

She didn't let go of his hand until they reached the refreshment table where Jackson was waiting. "This is my daddy, Austin Miller. And this is Jackson, my new friend. Did I do it right, Daddy?"

"You did a perfect job." Austin smiled down at her.

From where Tracey was standing, behind a fake ficus tree, she could see and hear every word, and the love that Austin had for his daughter gave her heart a shot of jealousy and one of regret at the same time. Jackson should be knowing that kind of fatherly love, but because she had been spoiled, her son had to go through life without a father.

Jackson wiped icing from a cookie on his blue trousers and stuck out his hand. "I'm pleased to meet you, sir. Emily says you're the best daddy in the whole world. I don't have a daddy, but I've got a Poppa Frank and he's the best grandfather in the whole world. I sure do like those boots."

"Pleased to meet you, too, son. So your mommy is Tracey Walker, is she? I used to know her a long time ago." Austin squatted down so he could look Jackson in the face.

Tracey held her breath so long that her chest ached before she finally let it out in a whoosh that shook dust from the ficus tree.

"Yep. Where'd you get those boots, anyway?" Jackson scanned the room and lowered his voice to a whisper. "I'm going to see Poppa Frank today, and I'm going to tell him I want some boots and a pair of jeans like yours. But don't tell Mommy because she gets real mad if I ask Poppa Frank for anything. He says she worries about money too much."

You little scamp. Tracey smiled.

"I won't tell her," Austin whispered back seriously as he straightened up and took his daughter's hand in his. "Emily, I think maybe it's time for us to be going. Granny will be wonderin' where we are, and you need to groom your pony. She hasn't been brushed all week."

"Can Jackson come to Granny's with me, Daddy? I told him he could come and pet Maybelle. I bet he could help brush her, too," Emily begged.

"Maybe another time," Austin answered and then turned to speak to Jackson. "You'll have to ask your mom if she'll bring you to Tom Bean, Texas, to see Emily's pony, Maybelle."

"Wow! That would be awesome!" Jackson said and looked around the room again "But wait a minute. Where do I tell Poppa Frank to take me to get some boots like yours?"

Austin patted him on the head. "Try a western wear store, son, like Sheplers."

You don't have the right to call Jackson son, Tracy thought. *But truth be told, that's on me, not on you.*

Austin was coming right toward her, and he had that look on his face that she recognized from years before. She stepped out from behind her hiding place and met him halfway, bracing herself for the inevitable storm.

"Tracey." He raised an eyebrow.

"Austin." She managed a smile. "This must be your daughter and Jackson's best friend."

Emily put a hand over her mouth and giggled. "The teacher thought you were my mama 'cause we both got red hair." Then she removed her hand and became serious. "Can Austin come to the ranch with me sometime and meet my pony? Her name is Maybelle, and I know she would like him."

"Maybe someday," Tracey said, "but we're going to see his grandpa today."

"We should talk," Austin whispered.

"Later," she told him. "Y'all have a good weekend, and it was very nice to meet you, Emily."

The little girl did a curtsy and said, "It was nice to meet you, ma'am." Then she looked up at Austin and asked, "Did I do that right, too, Daddy?"

"You were perfect," Austin said.

Austin shot another of those looks over his shoulder as he and Emily disappeared out the door.

Jackson ran over to her and put his small hand in hers. "I was lookin' and lookin' for you, Mama. Did you see Emily? She says that I can come meet her pony someday if it's all right with you." Jackson skipped along beside his mother. "Did we do good in the play? Could you hear me when I said my part?"

"It was a great party, and you were awesome onstage," Tracey assured him as she opened the back door to her car and got him strapped in. "I was so proud of you. You'll have to tell Poppa Frank all about it, and maybe even recite your lines to him."

"I can do that," Jackson told her. "Did you pack Woof-Woof and Cowboy Bear?"

"They're both in the truck with our luggage, and you've got a tote bag full of books on the seat beside you," Tracey answered.

Woof-Woof was a big stuffed dog that had been bigger than he was when Tracey's father gave it to Jackson for his first Christmas. Cowboy Bear was a small teddy bear that had come with plastic cowboy boots and a Stetson hat. Her dad had bought it, too, a year ago when Jackson decided to like all things cowboy.

"I'm going to show Emily Woof-Woof and Cowboy Bear when she comes to see me," he said as he dug around in the tote bag and brought out a book about cowboys.

"I bet she'll like both of them." Tracey sighed.

"I liked her daddy a whole lot. He wears awesome boots," Jackson said, "just like the cowboy in my book. I bet he's got a hat like this, too."

He used to have, Tracey thought. *A black Stetson that he always wore when we went dancing.*

A shiver chased down her back when she remembered how she had felt in his arms back then. Every woman in the country bar had looked at her with envy, and she loved it.

"Lots of the boys at school have boots, and they wear jeans just like his," Jackson went on. "Look, Mama, there's guys fishin' out there." He pointed to the water below them as they crossed the bridge over Lake Texoma.

Thank you, Lord, for distracting him away from boots and hats like Austin wears. Tracey sent up a silent prayer.

"I wonder if Emily's daddy has a boat like that. If he does, maybe he'll take me and Emily fishin'." Jackson sighed.

"So much for distractions," Tracey muttered.

Jackson went back to looking through his books, and soon he had propped his pillow up against the door and fallen asleep.

"He's probably dreaming of ponies, fishing, cowboy hats and boots, and Austin," she whispered. "I just hope I was imaging the connection between them."

Tracey's thoughts turned back to the look on Austin's face when he realized that his daughter's brand-new friend was Tracey's son. Surely, he hadn't put two and two together and come up with four. She had been so careful about Jackson's father. Not even her father knew it was Austin, and that's the way she intended to keep things. The kids might be best friends now, but they would forget each other, because in a year Tracey would be gone. She didn't care if she had to go back to teaching high school, like she had when she was taking online graduate courses. She turned on the radio to her favorite country-music station and turned the volume down low so it wouldn't wake Jackson. To take her mind off Austin and the way he looked at his daughter that evening, she sang along with Miranda Lambert to "Storms Never Last." She tapped out the rhythm on the steering wheel with her thumb.

"I remember a time when Austin's hand in mine really did still the thunder," she muttered, "but now all I can hope for is that this new storm will be over soon, and he hasn't figured out that Jackson is his son."

Tracey wondered about the girl he had left her for and married. Why did she leave him? And what kind of mother would walk off and leave her child?

She was so deep in thought that she missed the first exit to Purcell and had to drive four more miles to the next one. She was glad that Jackson was still sleeping when they passed McDonald's or he would have wanted a kid's meal—hamburger, fries, and milk, and of course the toy that came in the bag.

He didn't wake up until she turned into the driveway at her father's house. Another Miranda song, "The House That Built Me," went through her mind as she parked behind her father's vehicle. This was the house that her parents brought her home to when she was born. There was a room upstairs that hadn't been redecorated or touched since she left when she was six months pregnant with Jackson.

Jackson rubbed his eyes with his fists and said, "Are we there yet, Mama?"

"We *are* here, and Molly is waiting at the door," Tracey answered.

Jackson ran into Molly's open arms. "I missed y'all, but I got a new friend. Her name is Emily, and someday I'm going to ask her daddy if she can come home with me to see y'all. I'm hungry, Molly. What's for supper?"

Jackson broke away from Molly's hug and yelled. "Poppa! Poppa Frank, where are you?"

"Right here, son." Frank Walker stepped out on the porch and picked Jackson up and held him tightly against his chest. "Why did you take so long to get here? Has your mother started driving slow?"

"Nope, Poppa Frank, she's still hell on wheels. Whoops! Sorry, Mommy." Jackson clapped his hand over his mouth. "I'm not supposed to say that word. She says I can't say that word just because you say it. But she drove real fast. I shut my eyes, and then we were here. Is supper ready? Did Molly make biscuits and gravy, too? Mommy can't make gravy as good as yours."

"Boy, you ask more questions than a sane person can answer in a hundred years."

Jackson chuckled.

"You go on inside and check out that supper Molly has made for us, and I'll help your mama bring in the baggage."

Tracey's father met her at the back of the car and gave her a hug. "I missed you. Even though it's just been a week, that's too long to be way from you and Jackson."

"I agree, Daddy," Tracey said, "and I'm glad for a three-day weekend so we can come home and relax."

Frank picked up a suitcase with one hand and tucked the huge stuffed dog under his other arm. "I missed Woof-Woof, too," he said with a grin.

Tracey noticed a few more gray hairs scattered in her father's dark-brown hair. His mossy-green eyes looked tired, but then it was Friday. He had probably had a long week at the firm.

"Don't lollygag out there." Molly appeared in the open door again. "Supper is ready to put on the table."

"We're on the way," Tracey said with a grin, "but save me a hug. Don't give them all to Jackson."

"I keep plenty of hugs just for you, darlin' girl," Molly said.

Tracey set a suitcase and Cowboy Bear down in the foyer, slung her arm around the housekeeper's shoulders, and the two of them went in the house together.

When the hug ended, Molly folded her arms over her chest and narrowed her dark-brown eyes as she checked Tracey out from head to toe. "What's bothering you?"

"Nothing." Tracey fought the impulse to cross her fingers behind her back. "It's just been a long week, and I'm happy to be home."

"Mmm...huh." Molly tucked an errant stand of hair back into the gray bun on top of her head. "We'll talk about this later. Right now, you need a good hot supper and a night's rest."

The dining room table had seen lots of entertaining when Tracey's mother was alive. Every holiday had been an occasion for a party and for Frank Walker to show off his gorgeous wife, but these days the most entertaining that happened in the Walker house was when Jackson and Tracey came for a visit.

"Do you think God gave chickens two legs because He knew I liked fried chicken legs?" Jackson sat on his grandfather's right side with Tracey beside him.

Molly smiled across the table. "Well, sweet boy, this chicken had six legs just in case you and your Poppa Frank didn't get full on just two each." She passed the platter to Frank.

"Oh, Molly, you know chickens only got two legs." Jackson giggled. "We had a party today at school, Poppa Frank. I'll sing the songs and tell you and Molly what I said after supper." He put a spoonful of mashed potatoes covered with milk gravy in his mouth.

"I can't wait to hear all that," Frank said.

Jackson took a bite of his mashed potatoes and gravy and rolled his eyes toward the ceiling. "Molly, did you make this, or did God make it?" he asked Molly with a grin. "It's so good it must've been cooked in heaven!"

"You're a little charmer, you are." Molly laughed with him.

"I got a new friend, Poppa Frank. Her name is Emily and she's a girl. She's got a pony and today I met her daddy and I want—" He glanced over at Tracey. "I'm not supposed to ask you for things, but I hate my britches. The other boys in my school wear jeans, and"—he took a deep breath and avoided his mother's eyes—"some of them wear cowboy boots."

"Is that right?" his grandfather inquired seriously.

"I want some cowboy jeans and cowboy boots like Emily's daddy wears. He said to tell you we can buy them at any western store. I want them to be long enough to stack up over my boots. That's what Emily says cowboys call it when their jeans bunch up like that."

"Jackson Walker!" Tracey scolded.

"Wait a minute." Frank held up one hand toward her. "You must like Emily's daddy a whole lot, huh?"

"I don't know if I like him a whole lot or not. I only saw him today. But I liked his clothes. I don't want to wear these stupid slacks with pleats, and I don't like these shoes, Poppa Frank. I want to look like the other boys." Jackson still wouldn't look at his mother.

"Well then. Maybe we'll go shopping tomorrow. Just you and me. What kind of boots did you say they were?" he asked with a wink.

"Emily says they're Ropers and all the Texans in Tom Bean wear them. She says she wears hers when she rides her pony. I'm goin' to Tom Bean someday and I want a pair so I can ride that pony. Maybelle, that's her pony, might not like me if I don't have some Roper boots on, Poppa Frank. And I want to ride Maybelle more'n anything in the whole world."

"Then eat your supper and then we'll watch *Lion King* again tonight after you sing and tell us your poem. Tomorrow we'll go to Oklahoma City. I bet they've got some jeans and a pair of boots in your size just waiting for you," Frank said.

"Daddy?" Tracey raised an eyebrow.

"I won't have him bullied because he's not dressed like the rest of the kids. Either you take him, or he and I will go." Frank's tone did not leave room for argument.

After the month Tracey had had, she didn't have the energy to argue. "Thank you. I'm sure he would far rather make it a guys' day."

Even though Molly pressured her several times throughout the weekend for answers as to what she was worrying about, Tracey put her off by saying she was just tired. By Monday evening, she was almost glad to leave and go back to her apartment in Durant. And for the first time ever, Jackson was happy to go home. He had five pair of new jeans that Molly had washed and ironed for him, five western shirts, and two pairs of boots. Next time, Tracey swore, she would go with her father and son when they went on a shopping trip for new clothes.

"I'll find out what's going on next time you come home," Molly whispered as she hugged Tracey goodbye that evening.

"It's just the stress of a new job," Tracey assured her, even if she didn't believe it herself.

Frank gave her a hug and helped her load everything into the trunk of her car. "Send me a picture of him tomorrow in his new duds," he said.

"I'll do it," Tracey promised, "and I'll call or text when we get home."

"I'll be looking for it," Frank said.

When she started the engine and pulled away from the driveway, she watched Molly and her father wave from the porch until she was out of sight.

"Mama, you can drive like a bat..." Jackson slapped a hand over his mouth.

"Why do you want to get home so fast?" Tracey asked as she left the driveway.

"'Cause then pretty soon it will be bedtime, and then I can wake up and go to school in my new boots," he said. "Maybe Emily's daddy will come get her tomorrow before you get there, and I can show them to him."

It's begun, Tracey thought, *and all I can do is pray that I can keep my secret.*

Chapter 6

ON TUESDAY AFTERNOON, WHEN HER LAST CLASS HAD FIN-
ished, Tracey heaved a sigh of relief that she hadn't seen
Austin all day. She left her door open, set her briefcase on
the floor beside her desk, and went to the back of the room
to look out the window at the center of the campus. Students
were scurrying around, some going toward the parking lot,
some toward the library, and a few were clumped in groups,
laughing and gesturing with their hands.

She heard the door between her office and Austin's open,
and she didn't have to turn around to know that he was in
the room. The same vibes that she had felt when they were
together settled over her like a warm blanket on a cold
winter night. She spun around to find him standing in the
doorway between their offices with his arms crossed over his

chest, eyebrows drawn down and one leg crossed over the other one.

He looked long, lean, sexy as hell—just like he had that night when they'd had the argument that ended in disaster. He had the same expression he'd had on that rainy night, too.

Well, he can stay like that until his foot goes to sleep and he falls on his face, or until his face freezes in that position. I am not starting this conversation.

"Trace?" he finally said.

"Austin?" she said right back in the same cool tone.

"We need to talk," he said.

"You can talk. I'll listen." She sat down in the chair behind her desk and crossed her legs.

He drew his dark brows down in a frown, but even with that expression on his sculpted face, he was still so sexy that he jacked up her pulse.

"All right, have it your way." He grabbed a folding chair from the other side of the desk, snapped it open, and sat down so close that their knees were touching.

Even through his thick jeans, his touch caused her heart to skip a beat and then race ahead with a full head of steam.

"Let's go back six years. I was furious at you that night. You were acting so damned spoiled, but I loved you so much.

I knew I could never, ever give you all the things you were used to having. But I still wanted you. I just was determined not to let your daddy pick up the bills the way you wanted him to."

"I did not!"

"Well, you weren't making any attempts to be self-supporting. And you knew we'd be living on a teacher's salary once we were married," he pointed out.

Tracey let out the breath she'd been holding. "Austin, what went on six years ago is in the past. Let it go."

"I thought you were being stubborn because deep down inside, you didn't want to get married. The money I was earning that month we were out for break had already been earmarked for the next semester's tuition because my scholarship had run out." He leaned forward. "Don't tune me out, Trace. I need to explain to you what happened."

She willed the tears welling up not to fall down her cheeks. "If it will make you feel any better or bring closure to you, then explain away." She checked the time on her cell phone. "You've got about fifteen minutes before we go pick up our children at school."

"When I got home, I ran into a bunch of my old high school buddies and they invited me to go out with them. We started drinking. First, it was a couple of beers, then someone bought a fifth and we started drinking boilermakers. The next mornin', I woke up in the back bedroom of a trailer house with Crystal Smith. She was eighteen years old and wild as a March hare. Everyone else had left long since, but I stayed with her for three days before I sobered up and went home."

"What a romantic story," Tracey whispered. "Do I really have to know all this?"

"Yes. You do," Austin said. "It wasn't long before she started getting sick in the mornings. She knew she was pregnant, and I knew it, too. She wanted to get an abortion and wanted me to pay for it, but you know my views on that. So I talked her into marryin' me. I swore I'd forget you and make a home for the baby and for Crystal. I guess I thought she'd straighten up and become a sweet little wife and mother when the baby was born. I was a fool. She turned around all right, but it was for the worse. She told me she hated my guts for getting her pregnant. She slept on the couch and said she didn't want me to touch her. All she wanted was a divorce and an abortion." His voice cracked.

"Austin, I—"

"No." He held up one hand. "I want you to hear the whole story. Four months after we were married, I came home from work and she was gone. There was a note on the table. She'd gone off with her old boyfriend. A truck driver named Bubba. She wrote that I could do whatever I damn well pleased."

"What did you do?" Tracey asked.

"I moved back home. I got a letter in June from somewhere in Maine. She said that she'd gone in for an abortion, but the clinic said she was too far along and she'd let me know when the baby was born. In August, I got another letter from Nevada that said she had gotten a divorce from me in that state. On September 23, she called me from Denison and said she was in the hospital there. She said she'd just had a baby girl, and they were discharging her the next day. She said she had put my name down as father, but she hadn't named the baby. They were going to dismiss her the next day, and it was up to me if I wanted the kid or if I wanted to sign my parental rights away and let her be put up for adoption. If I wanted to keep the kid, as she kept calling the new baby, then to bring a car seat and something to put on her to take her home. I was at the hospital at ten o'clock the next mornin'."

"Good grief!" Tracey shivered.

"I was there. She handed me the baby with a paper she had written up and had notarized about how she didn't want this child and never, ever wanted to see it or me again. Bubba picked her up and helped her into the truck and they drove off together. I just stood there with this eight-pound baby girl in my arms. My mother went with me and helped me pick out a little outfit and a blanket to take her home in. The next day I went to a lawyer, and the next time Crystal and Bubba came through town to see her folks, Crystal signed the papers that officially gave me sole custody of Emily. I hear she and Bubba settled down somewhere in California where he's still driving a truck. She's never called or written Emily, so I guess she meant it when she said she didn't want her."

"Poor, poor baby." Tracey couldn't believe any mother could be so cold.

"I found out that a single parent could get a lot of government help to finish school. I applied for it. Emily and I moved to Durant, and I quit my job in Texas. I went back to college and finished the next year. Momma wanted me to leave Emily in Tom Bean, but I couldn't. She was my child, my responsibility, and besides, I wanted to come home at night to her. I wanted to be the first one to see her walk, the first one to know she'd cut a tooth. I wanted her to run to me when she scraped her knee, not to my mother."

"I understand." Tracey nodded.

"I had a degree and the university administration let me

teach here while I got my master's. I started out teaching Comp I, like you, and moved up to Comp II and American Literature a couple of years ago," he explained.

"What did Crystal look like?" she asked.

"She was five feet three inches tall, shorter than you. She had the same color hair you do. That's why the teacher's aide thought you were Emily's mother. I haven't seen her since the day she gave up her rights to Emily."

"You didn't tell Emily that her mother didn't want her, did you?" Tracey asked.

"No. I told her that her mother gave her to me to raise because she married a truck driver and didn't have a house or a place to keep a pony," Austin answered. "Why didn't you tell me about Jackson?"

"Why didn't you call and tell me all this when it happened?" she asked.

"I tried. Your phone line was disconnected. Your father's phone is unlisted. I drove to Purcell and asked directions to Frank Walker's house at a service station. They told me how to get there, but when I knocked on the door, no one answered. I didn't even know if I had the right place," he answered.

If we were meant to be together, someone would have been home, she thought.

Silence as thick as a heavy fog filled the room. Neither of them said a word for several minutes, and then finally Austin broke the silence. "Are you going to answer me?"

"You walked out. You went on a drunken binge for three days. Then you married a girl you hardly knew." She turned her face away from him.

"Good point." He nodded. "But you've robbed me of almost six years of knowing my son."

"*Your* son!" she exploded. "What gives you the right or reason to say Jackson is your son? Jackson belongs to me! I had him after twenty-four hours of labor. I didn't walk out of the hospital and give him away. I've loved him and I've done it all on my own, without help from anyone." This time she couldn't keep the tears from streaming down her cheeks.

"I know that. I met your father in Oklahoma City last night for supper. He told me how well you've done on your own. And there was pure pride in his voice." Austin pulled a tissue from the box on her desk and handed it to her.

"You talked to my father?" She dabbed at her eyes.

"Yes, I did. It didn't take a mathematical genius to know how long it takes to produce a baby. Jackson was born on September 13, according to Emily. They think it's great that they were born the same month. That makes him just ten days older than she is. I know that Jackson is my son. What I don't know is why you didn't tell me."

"Why in the hell did you talk to my father? Did you tell him you thought you were Jackson's father?" Her voice was about to crack even in her own ears.

"You want to know how I got his unlisted number? Jackson wrote it down on a piece of paper for Emily so she could call him at his Poppa Frank's house over the weekend," he said, "and yes, I told Frank, but he said he had known it from the beginning. I told him the same story I just told you. After he got through telling me what a fool I had been and how he wanted to shoot me and I apologized for being an idiot, we had a long man-to-man talk."

"Why? Why couldn't you just leave us alone?"

"Because I've never stopped thinking about you, Trace. And I want to know my son. From the minute I laid eyes on him when Emily introduced us last Friday, I knew in my heart he was mine. You can't deny it. He has my eyes, and he's already taller than the kids in their class, just like I was when I was his age."

"B-but—" Tracey stammered.

"I guess that he doesn't know about me, and I'm a patient man these days. Being a single parent has taught me that. I'll let you decide when to tell him about me, but I won't wait until he's a grown man, Trace. I plan to be a part of his life." Austin straightened up in the chair, but their knees were still touching.

"I put 'father unknown' on his birth certificate," she admitted.

"That's just paper. We both know the truth. I'll give you a week or two to think about what I've said, and then we can figure out what to do." He shook the legs of his jeans down when he stood up. "By the way, Trace, I've never stopped loving you. But we can talk about that later."

Austin unlocked and opened the door to the hallway and went through the adjoining door to his office, leaving it ajar. He stuck his head back around and added, "Oh yeah. I saw Jackson when I took Emily to school this morning. He came running from across the playground to show me his new boots. And I forgot to tell you that I appreciate that you gave him my middle name—Nelson. Emily's full name is Emily Trace Miller. Not Tracey. Just Trace, like I've always called you. And for your information, I didn't hack into the school records to find that out. Emily told me."

"You named your little girl for me?" Tracey asked in a voice just above a whisper. "Why would her mother let you do that?"

"She was Baby Girl Miller when Crystal handed her over to me. Any more questions?"

Tracey shook her head. Questions came with answers, and she didn't want to know anymore. The prospect of introducing Jackson to his real father at long last was unsettling enough. Although she had an uncomfortable feeling her son would be thrilled, that would mean letting Austin back into her life in some measure, as well as Jackson's.

Austin came back in the room, put the chair back where he had gotten it, and turned around just before he reached the door. "Tracey?"

"What?" She checked the time. She still had five minutes, and she would need every second of that time to calm herself.

"You did a real fine job of raising our boy. I'm not looking to take him away from you. Right now, I just want him to know he's got a father. We can work out the details as we go along. So don't get your feathers up." He winked.

"Oh!" She picked up a textbook to toss at him, but Austin had already closed the door behind him. The heavy book fell to the floor with a thud.

Tracey was overwhelmed, but she had to compartmentalize everything and go get her son. When she reached the school,

Jackson was playing on the merry-go-round. "Mama"—he waved at her—"come push me."

"We should be getting home," she said.

"Just one time," Jackson begged, "and then you can sit down and ride with me. Emily already went home, but her daddy pushed me and her one time. He said he liked my jeans and boots."

"Just one time," she agreed, hoping that when Jackson found out who his father was, it wouldn't change the relationship she had with him. She gave the merry-go-round a hard push and sat down on it.

Jackson squealed and enjoyed the ride. Why did life have to be so complicated? It had been just her and Jackson for so long.

Austin was more than just a patient man, but he wouldn't wait forever. He'd said that much.

But she wouldn't worry about that today. This was a moment of freedom with Jackson, with the wind blowing through her red hair and his that was as dark as Austin's. When the merry-go-round came to a slow stop, Tracey got off and gave it another spin. "That first one was for you, and this one is for me," she told Jackson, "but when it stops, we really do have to go home."

"Make it go fast, like a bat out of hell, Mom," Jackson said.

Tracey gave it a hard spin and sat down again. He had called her Mom—not Mommy, but Mom. Today of all days was not the day for him to grow up and call her Mom.

The merry-go-round came to a stop, and Jackson didn't argue about going home—not when he saw Emily and Austin walking across the playground toward them.

"Hey, Jackson," she called out and came running toward him. "I forgot my lunch box, and me and Daddy came back to get it."

The little girl stopped so fast that dust boiled up around her boots that were almost identical to the Ropers that Jackson was wearing. She looked Tracey right in the eye and started to say something, but then Austin caught up to her.

"We need to get inside the room and get your lunch pail, sweetheart, before the teacher leaves," he said.

"Just a minute, Daddy," Emily said. "I need to talk to Jackson's mom." She focused on Tracey again and smiled. "You are so pretty. I want to know where you buy your dresses and skirts. Granny said she would take me shopping for girl stuff. Not like my Sunday clothes, but school things, but I don't want to go to the western store."

"I bet she could find what you want in the mall. They

have several stores that have little girls' things. And thank you for saying I'm pretty. I've been feeling a little bit unfashionable," she said.

"Oh, no, ma'am." Emily shook her curls. "You're just perfect."

"I can agree with that." Austin winked again. "But you need to run along now and get your lunch pail."

"Come on, Jackson." Emily grabbed his hand. "You can go with me."

They took off, hand in hand, toward the classroom.

"What're the odds?" Austin asked.

"One in a trillion," Tracey answered.

"I'd pay you to take her shopping sometime this week," Austin said. "I guess I have bought most of her things in the western store, but when we're not in Durant, we are on the ranch at my folks' house. Mama told me I was turning her into a tomboy, but…" He shrugged.

"She's going to tell you what she wants, and I'll bet it will be mostly what she sees the other little girls wearing to school. That's why Jackson has jeans and boots. He wants to look like the other boys in his room," Tracey said even though she would have loved to go shopping for girlie things with the child.

"She does have a mind of her own," Austin said.

"That's a good thing," Tracey told him.

The kids came racing across the playground, and both of them carried a lunch pail in their hands.

"Guess what, Mom," Jackson said. "I had forgotted mine, too."

Emily put her small hand in Austin's and said, "Bye, Jackson. Don't forget to ask your mom about the party!"

"What party?" Tracey asked him when they reached the car and Jackson was strapped into his booster seat.

"Me and Emily has both got birthdays pretty soon. We want to have a party together," he told her. "We could go to the pizza place or to McDonald's and then go play in the park, and"—he took a deep breath—"maybe after that we could go to Tom Bean and I could see Maybelle."

"Has Emily talked to her daddy about this?" she asked.

"Nope, not yet. We just thought it up today," he said. "I'm hungry. Let's go home and fix some s'ghetti for supper. And some of that long, skinny bread you put that shaky cheese on, and a big old root beer. I'm so hungry I could eat a horse!"

"Could you eat Maybelle?" she asked.

"Nope. Maybelle's not for eating, she's for riding. Riding in my new boots and my new jeans with Emily right up there beside me," he said proudly. "Emily said she'd ride with me at first, so I won't be scared. But I will be. For just a little bit I'll be scared, Mom, because I'll be riding for the first time. But that's all right, ain't it?"

"Isn't it," she corrected. "Yes, it's all right to be scared. Even mommies get scared sometimes." Right now, the mere thought of telling Jackson that Austin Miller was his father scared her half to death.

As soon as she and Jackson were in their apartment, she went into her bedroom and changed into a pair of worn gray sweatpants and a T-shirt with a faded picture of Minnie Mouse on the front.

When she found out she was pregnant with Jackson, Austin accusing her of being spoiled and not making her own way had kept haunting her, so she had made up her mind to prove him wrong. She had moved out of her father's house into a small apartment, gotten a job as a tutor on campus, and done some data processing at night for a couple of professors. And she had refused to let her father help her with anything. She had even slept on the floor on a mattress until she could buy an iron bed frame at a garage sale. She'd stripped off all the old paint and rust and repainted it sunshine yellow. The same yellow paint had freshened up a ten-drawer dresser that a teacher friend had passed along. Over it hung an unusual mirror of her own design made from an old six-paned window. She'd had the broken glass removed and replaced with six small panes of mirrored glass and painted the frame emerald green.

Jackson still loved seeing six reflections of himself in it when he could talk her into holding him up high enough to do it. She had rocked Jackson to sleep many nights in the old green rocker over there in the corner of her bedroom. Now he was too big for her lap.

She caught her own reflection in the six-paned mirror. She'd aged in the past six years, but then so had Austin. She leaned in and studied her reflection for wrinkles and only found a few tiny crow's-feet around her eyes.

"I guess there's something all women aren't happy with," she said. "Mine is that I wish I could erase these freckles."

"Hey, Mom," Jackson called from his bedroom. "Come see this. There's a spider with real long legs right here on my bed."

She hated spiders more than anything, but if one was about to bite her son, she would damn sure send it off to that great web in the sky.

"Where?" she asked from the door to his room. There

was a set of twin beds covered with bright-red spreads. The beds she had rescued from beside the dumpsters outside her apartment in Purcell, and the spreads were another garage sale find. The beds were separated by the chest of drawers he'd had since he was a baby. She'd bought it at an unfinished furniture store and redone it herself, rubbing maple stain into the wood and then sealing it before coating it twice with spar varnish to make it watertight.

"Where is this monster spider?" she asked.

Jackson pointed to the spare bed. "Don't kill it. That kind of spider only eats bugs. We learned about it in school today," he said. "Just get a grocery sack and scare it in it and then put it outside. I bet he heard us talking about s'ghetti and he thought he'd come to supper."

She got a paper sack from the kitchen, chased the spider into it, and took it down the stairs to the courtyard where she turned it loose. She was on her way back up the stairs when she heard a pickup truck. When she reached the landing, she heard giggles and turned around to take a look. Her chest tightened and she dropped the now-empty paper sack. The wind picked it up and blew it against the wrought-iron railing.

Austin had promised to give her a couple of weeks to think

things over, not a couple of hours, and he certainly didn't need to bring Emily with him. She was frozen even though the breeze was hot against her face.

Austin wasn't walking toward her, but he was opening the door to an apartment on the ground floor right across from her. How had she never seen him here before?

Because, the niggling voice in her head reminded her, *you park your car behind your apartment and usually take the back stairs when you leave. And he's teaching that early morning class this semester, so he leaves an hour earlier than you do.*

"Oh, great," she said out loud.

"Hey, Mom." Jackson came out onto the landing. "Did the spider make it out of the sack okay?"

"Shh," she whispered loudly. "Go on back in the apartment or he'll hear you."

"Okay," he mouthed and minded her for the first time in months without a whole bevy of questions.

Chapter 7

TRACEY UNSNAPPED HER BRIEFCASE AND TOOK OUT HER trusty red pen and the first of thirty-five compositions from her 8:00 a.m. class. She'd asked them to write about a person or place that had influenced their decision to go to college, and she'd wanted it in hard copy.

She picked up the first paper, read the opening sentence, and looked up at the wall in the dining room, where she sat at the bistro table for two with the stacks of papers in front of her. There was a poster-size photo of Jackson taken just last year in the garden behind her father's house. He was smiling and waving, and Tracey smiled back at the photo absentmindedly.

Lost in reverie, she continued to look at it for at least ten minutes before she realized she wasn't focusing but worrying about Austin living in the same complex that she did. She went to the living room window and opened it a few inches. The night air smelled wonderful, and stars as bright as diamonds glittered in the black sky. A frog sang the blues off in the distance, and she could hear a few crickets trying to harmonize with him. Then someone cleared his throat and she looked down to see Austin standing on his tiny porch, looking up at the same stars she was admiring. Tracey suddenly felt a desperate need to talk to him. Really talk...and really listen. She checked Jackson to make sure he was sleeping soundly and slipped out the front door. Changing from sweatpants, T-shirt, and house shoes into something nicer didn't enter her mind. She didn't care if her hair was straggling down curls around her neck and face. She wasn't going over there to flirt, but to let him know that they were living in the same complex.

Tracey walked right up on his porch.

"Trace?

"Can we talk, out here in the courtyard?" she asked. "I left Jackson asleep, and I want to be able to keep an eye on the door."

"What are you talking about? What door? Where'd you come from?" he asked.

"Up there." She nodded toward the apartment with the open drapes. The light from the window shone down on the courtyard. "I live up there. I didn't know you lived here until this evening. I was outside setting a spider free when you and Emily came home."

"Well, I'll be damned." He flashed a bright smile. "You mean to say you've lived there a whole month without me knowin' it?"

"Yes. Believe me, I wouldn't have moved into this complex if I'd known..." she stammered. "I just wanted you to know—for the kids' sake. I'm surprised they didn't already figure it out since they know so much about each other."

"That's the truth," he said. "Want a beer or a bottle of sweet tea?"

"No, I just wanted to—" She started and stopped again. "Tell you that I've decided to tell Jackson about you in a few days. By myself. He already likes you. I want to do the right thing, Austin, I really do."

"Thanks, Trace." He nodded.

"How is Emily going to feel about this? She's had you all to herself for a long time, and she has no idea Jackson is her brother." Tracey was having a change of heart as she thought about the effect this would have on both children. "Maybe it would be best to tell them at the same time so there won't be any surprises for her either. I'm drowning here with all the decisions."

"I'll abide by whatever you think is best," Austin said.

"Emily might also feel upset about something else," Tracey said. "Jackson is going to have a father and a mother, and all she's got is a father. Up till now they've been equal. Jackson has a mother and she's got a father. One of each, you know." Tracey tried to explain—as much or more to herself than to Austin.

"We'll figure it all out," Austin said. "But something else is bothering you. Remember, I know you, Trace."

"Your daughter is adorable, but they've both been only children until now. What about when there is competition between them?" Tracey asked. "It will happen. They're just little kids. How are you going to feel the first time Emily accuses you of loving Jackson more than her because he has hair like yours or because he's a boy?"

"We'll cross that bridge when we come to it," he answered. "But I still don't think that's what's on your mind."

Tracey didn't want to say any more that night, but he deserved the truth. "I'm afraid that when I look at her, I won't see the wonderful little girl she is. I'm afraid I might resent her because you chose her mother over me." Tracey looked up at him. She was standing close enough that she could see the five-o'clock shadow of his beard, dark from the porch light.

"I can understand that, too," he said. "But you've got to admit, I chose Crystal at a time when I didn't even know you were pregnant. I was young and stupid and thought I was doing the right thing when I married her."

"Okay…" She drew out the word. "But it doesn't change the past or shape the future. I'll try to handle you being a part of Jackson's life, but I'm not sure I can ever be a part of Emily's."

"I see," Austin said slowly. "Let me ask you something, Trace. Where do I stand in all this? Are you seeing someone else? Have you been married? There's a lot of questions I'd like to ask about these past six years."

"I'm not married. Haven't ever been. I'm not seeing anyone right now. Where do you want to stand?"

"I told you today." Austin raked his hand through his hair.

"How can you still love me?" she said. "You haven't seen or talked to me in years."

"Time doesn't erase real love," he answered. "I'm hoping

that someday you'll forgive me and love me back. But I won't pressure you. Right now, I'm just grateful that you'll let me be a part of Jackson's life." He laid his hand on her shoulder and gave it a gentle squeeze.

The warm night and his soft tone put her in mind of their first weeks together, when she'd been young enough to believe that love conquered all. But her life was a whole lot more complicated now. She needed time—a lot of time—to think. Admitting to Austin that she was willing to let him be a part of Jackson's life was enough for this day.

"No strings attached?" she asked hesitantly. She didn't move her hand.

"None. My love is there for you. I can wait. When you decide what you want to do, let me know. We can go our separate ways or build some kind of relationship. Once upon a time, Trace...I loved you Red River deep. I still do. Don't forget that." His voice almost cracked.

But you walked out and left me all the same, Tracey thought miserably.

"I should be going," she said as she headed back across the courtyard. When she turned around at the top of the stairs, he held up a hand and waved.

Tracey waved back and went on inside to check on

Jackson. She stared down at his dark hair on the pillowcase with horses on it. She'd had her son all to herself for six wonderful years. He had the right to know his father. Austin was a good man and a great father to Emily, and Tracey knew down deep in her heart that he would be fair to both his children.

She wandered into the dining room once more and picked up the paper she had started to grade. This time she read it through and made several corrections in red pen. Surprising how easy it was to straighten out other people's mistakes. Too bad she couldn't fix her own with a red pen. Tracey picked up another paper and finished grading it. Before eleven o'clock, they were all finished, ready to give back to the students tomorrow for rewriting, and she was tired enough for bed.

A quick shower relaxed her, and she slipped on a cotton knit nightgown that had been blue once upon a time. Now it was almost white and there were splotches of red, pink, yellow, and purple finger paint from a rainy-day art project she and Jackson had done. The paint was supposed to be water soluble and wash right out of anything. It never had, but she liked the gown so well she kept wearing it even with the paint stains. Besides, it reminded her of a happy morning she'd spent with her son.

Tracey crawled into bed with a romance novel and read a chapter or two to make her sleepy. The hero was tall, strong, and dressed in faded jeans that fit him just so, and he had a way of walking that made the heroine sit up and take notice. She read a little more and realized the author could have been describing Austin. Yawning, she set the book aside, turned out the light, and fell into a sweet dream of her own hero holding her tight.

———————

"Hey, Mom," Jackson called out to her while they were getting dressed the next morning. "I want a big belt with a silver buckle for my birthday." He zipped his jeans and bent over to bunch the extra length around his boot. "You know, like Emily's dad has. Maybe you could find one with my initial engraved on it."

"You didn't tell Poppa Frank that's what you wanted, did you? I wouldn't want to get you the same thing you asked him for." She pulled on a pair of navy-blue dress slacks and a matching silk blouse and quickly buttoned up the front.

"Nope." He smiled. "I didn't ask Poppa Frank for a buckle."

His little-boy grin and the twinkle in his eye made her

think of Austin, and that made her think of the dream she'd had last night. Tracey blushed at the memory.

"Want to know what I asked Poppa Frank for?" Jackson's bright eyes seemed to beg her to ask him just what it was he wanted.

"I don't know." She played along. "Maybe you'd better not tell me, especially if it's a secret between you and Poppa Frank. Let me see, did you ask him for some more jeans?"

"No, silly. You know he bought me five pairs so I can have a clean pair every day and you can wash them all on Saturday."

"Don't remind me," Tracey said wryly. "I don't like to iron. Maybe I'll just take your jeans to that cleaners who gets things done in a day."

"Poppa Frank said to tell you to buy real starch and make creases down the legs when you iron them."

"I think on Friday evenings, we will take them to the cleaners." That would be a little extravagant, but well worth the money when she considered how cranky pressing five pairs of jeans would make her.

"I'm ready." Jackson grinned and slung his backpack over his shoulders.

Tracey picked up her briefcase and they walked out the door together.

"Guess again," Jackson said.

"Did you ask for another pair of boots? Are you really going to wear boots every single day of school?"

"Yep, Emily's daddy wears them every day and he's a teacher just like you, Mom. Anyway, I asked Poppa Frank for a pony," he answered as he opened the car door and got into his booster seat.

"A *what*?" Tracey gasped. "We can't keep a pony in an apartment complex, and Poppa Frank can't keep one in the backyard. He lives in town, Jackson Nelson Walker!"

"Poppa Frank said he'd have to talk to you first and find a place to keep her, but my Poppa Frank can fix anything," Jackson folded his arms across his chest and let a lungful of air out in a disappointed whoosh.

"Good mornin'." Austin was across the courtyard by his pickup. "How are you this mornin', Jackson?"

"Emily!" he shouted and waved out the open door. "How did you get here?"

"We live here, Jackson. How did you get here?" Emily left her father's side and ran over to Emily's car.

"I live here, too! Awesome! Hot damn, Emily, we live in the same place," he said.

"Jackson!" Tracey scolded.

"Well, Poppa Frank says 'hot damn' all the time and you don't holler at him." Jackson stuck his lip out and pouted.

"My uncle says it, too," Emily said. "But Daddy says it's a big-people word. Hey, we could play together since we live in the same place. You could come over to my apartment. Or we can play right here in the courtyard on the swings and jungle gym."

"Hey, Mom, can Emily ride to school with me today?" Jackson asked. "She can sit in the booster seat with me. There's plenty of room."

"Not today," Austin told him. "I have to talk to the teacher about something this morning. But if you'd like to ride with us and it's all right with your mom, then that would be fine. What do you say, Trace?" Austin flashed one of his bright smiles.

"Trace?" Emily said. "Is your name Trace? Mine is too. Emily Trace Miller. Everyone thinks it's a funny name," she said. "Do people think your name is funny, too?"

"Well, my name's Tracey, but your daddy has always called me Trace," she explained, hesitating only slightly.

"Oh, has my daddy known you for a long time?" Emily looked confused.

"Yes, he has," Tracey said.

"Well, my name is Jackson Nelson Walker, and that's my whole name," Jackson announced.

"That's awesome," Emily said. "My daddy's name is Austin Nelson Miller. I've got your mom's name and you got my dad's name. Jackson, come on, you can ride in the middle. If it's okay with your mom."

Austin raised an eyebrow.

"Okay, but you'll have to put his booster seat in the back seat of your truck," Tracey agreed. "Here's your lunch pail and your backpack. I'll pick you up as soon as school is over this afternoon."

"Thanks, Mom." Jackson gave her a hug and ran off to the pickup truck with Emily.

"Yeah, thanks, Trace," Austin said. "And I'll get the seat out of the back. I can't believe you're still driving this car."

"It still runs, and I don't have a car payment." She shrugged.

"Smart woman," Austin said.

―――――

Tracey didn't have plans for lunch, and she needed to get out for a while. Leaves from a few of the trees on campus had started to turn colors and fall. But being famous for its magnolia trees that stayed green, the campus pretty much looked the same all year long. When she had been there as a student, she didn't notice such things, but having an inquisitive little boy underfoot who asked questions about everything had taught her to pay closer attention. She walked two blocks down University Boulevard to a deli, bought a tuna salad sandwich and a diet soda, and took them back to her office. She ate her lunch by the window and tried to sort out her feelings.

Did she still love Austin? She had once thought she'd love him forever. Yet how could she not love him in some measure? Jackson was a physical miniature of his father, and she adored her son. "Penny for your thoughts," Austin said softly from the open doorway between their offices.

"Cost you more than that," she said without turning around. "I figured you'd be at lunch with one of those divorcées from the school who were panting after you at the party last week."

"I happen to prefer the red-haired professor who has this office. She was pretty nice to me this mornin' and I wanted to spend my lunch break with her. I got an apple. Want part of it?" He drew up a chair beside her, leaned back, and propped his feet on the windowsill.

"Nope, I'm having tuna salad," she said. "Did the kids behave?"

"Sure. I found out that two are easier than one. They entertained each other. She wants to see if he's got the same Star Wars stuff she has, and he wants to see what a Barbie doll looks like." Austin laughed. "He looks like me, doesn't he, Trace?"

"Yes, he does," she said. "Especially in those jeans and boots. He wants a silver belt buckle for his birthday. One with a J on it," she added.

"Would you mind if I bought it for him?" he asked. "That is, if you're goin' to tell him I'm his dad before his birthday."

"Seems like things are moving so fast," she said. "He'll be six a week from today. I thought I'd wait until after his birthday, so I could have one more with him when I didn't have to share him. But that's selfish, isn't it, Austin? I do want what's best for him."

"You can take this as slow as you want. We can wait until after his birthday, but maybe we could go to supper on his birthday and Emily and I can give him his buckle."

"That would be nice," she agreed. "He asked his Poppa Frank for a pony. I don't know where my dad plans to keep it. His place isn't right for a pony, and we wouldn't get up there often enough for Jackson to ride it very much."

"I told your dad he could keep the pony in Tom Bean with Maybelle, and Jackson could visit down there to ride it. That's up to you, too. You can discuss it with Frank when you call him later tonight," Austin said.

"How did you know I was going to talk to my daddy tonight?" she asked.

And how did you get to be on a first-name basis with him so fast? she wondered.

"He told me last night when we visited over the phone," Austin said.

"You've been talking to my dad?" She glared at him.

"Couple of times, ma'am," he said.

Tracey swiveled her chair around. "You two are really in cahoots, aren't you? Ever since you went and told him everything about you and me."

"I think your father actually likes me, Trace. He's called me a couple of times. Once to see about the pony, and another time to check on you."

Tracey had been on her own too long to feel comfortable with her father and Austin suddenly taking over her life so casually.

Austin put his chair back where he'd gotten it, grabbed her hand, and pulled her up into a hug and kissed her. He slid his tongue over her mouth, and she tasted fresh apple.

"I've wanted to do that since the first day you showed up here," he whispered.

His warm breath on her neck sent tingles down her spine, and when he drew her in for another kiss, she leaned into it. Then Tracey came to her senses and took a step back.

"What are you afraid of, Trace?"

"I'm not afraid. It's just that..." Tracey searched for the right words.

"It was just a couple of kisses," Austin said.

"This isn't the place, and this is way too fast."

Someone knocked on the door and turned the doorknob. Then a student poked her head in the door and said, "Miz Walker, I'm going to miss class this afternoon. I wanted to tell you that my paper has been turned in online."

"Thank you, Brenda," Tracey said. "I'm glad you got it done early."

The student waved and closed the door behind her.

"That was a close call," Tracey said. "But you can bet there will be rumors. From now on, when we're in either office alone, the door stays open."

"If that's what it takes." He shrugged.

Chapter 8

Tracey waited until Jackson was in bed and asleep before she made the phone call.

"Hello, Daddy."

"Hello, Tracey," he said.

There was silence on the other end of the line.

"I expect this call is about Austin Miller," her father said after a few heavy moments.

"Yes, it is," she said. "And I'm furious that you two had a just-us-men conversation behind my back. You could have let me know you were having dinner with him and that you have been calling him."

Frank Walker chuckled. "You can't be madder than I was when Jackson was born and you wouldn't tell me who his father was."

"So now you know," she said, "but Austin said that you told him you had always known, so why didn't you step up and admit it to me?"

"I knew two weeks after you wouldn't tell me back then," he admitted. "Detectives can find out anything in the whole damn world. When I got the whole story, I did my best to get you to come back home."

"You knew! All this time you knew! You hired someone to pry into my life?" She raised her voice a few octaves.

"Of course I knew. And I knew that he'd married another girl instead of you because she was pregnant, too. Besides, I'd obtained a copy of his college ID photo. When Jackson was a year old, I could see the resemblance, but after I found out Austin married that other girl, I let it drop. Figured you wouldn't want anything to do with him," he said.

"Did you know Austin was here in Durant when I took this teaching job?" she asked.

"No, I surely did *not*. Surprised the hell outta me when he called here and wanted to talk to me. I really like that man, Tracey, but we were going to talk about the pony, right?" He chuckled again.

"No, I'm not through talking about Austin," she hissed.

"Well, what else do you want to know? You know him a helluva lot better than I do anyway," he said.

"I'm mad at you," she said.

"You've been mad at me before and you got over it," Frank told her. "So let's talk about Austin some more. I'm a real good judge of character. He is a good man, and he told me he's always loved you and still does. Give him a chance. You never know what might happen. Now do you want to know about Buck?"

"Who?"

"Buck, the pony. I found a pretty little gelding pony," Frank said.

"What in the hell is a gelding?" Tracey asked.

"It's a male pony that's been castrated so it won't be a problem with Maybelle," he explained.

"So you know about Maybelle, too?" She tried to get a handle on her temper and control her voice.

"Of course I knew about Maybelle. I knew about her and Emily before I knew Emily was Austin's daughter. If you'll remember, when you were home for the long weekend, all Jackson talked about was his new friend and how she had a horse named Maybelle. That, and jeans and boots," he reminded her. "Austin says I can stable Buck down there in

Tom Bean with his daughter's horse, so I'll have him delivered there next weekend. On Jackson's birthday, I have to be out of town, so I'll call him and tell him all about the arrangements."

"Daddy, what am I going to do?" Tracey could hear the desperation in her own voice.

"Well, Austin's folks can feed Buck when they feed Maybelle, and then once or twice a week you take Jackson down there to brush the animal and let him ride it. I'll make arrangements to send them a monthly check for whatever feed they need for him," he answered.

"I'm not talking about the pony! I'm talking about Austin." She knew her father was teasing her.

"Oh, well, Austin is *your* problem. I can't tell you what to do about him. You and your heart have got to figure that out. If you love him, then I expect you'll know what to do. Oh, I hear Molly callin'. She says supper is ready," he said.

"At this time of night?" she asked.

"It's as good an excuse as any other." He chuckled again. "Good luck, honey. You've got a big job ahead of you. Teaching, and telling Jackson about his daddy, and figuring out whether or not to let Austin back in your life. And it's something you have to do on your own, just like you've had to prove your independence and raise that boy by yourself up until now. I'll call you over the weekend. Love you," he said and ended the call before she could say anything else.

━━━━━━━━

The rest of the week went by in a blur. She had a lunch engagement with Dr. Taylor on Wednesday and one with Dr. Benson on Thursday. Friday she and Twyla had a standing appointment for lunch at an all-you-can-eat pizza place on the west side of town. She had only seen Austin a couple of times in the hallway. He winked and waved, and once he paused just long enough to ask about Jackson and tell her he'd seen him at school when he picked Emily up.

Austin's truck was gone Saturday morning when she looked out the window. He had probably gone to Tom Bean to visit with his folks and let Emily see her pony. She wondered if he'd told his daughter that Jackson's pony was coming to live in the same place as Maybelle, and how Emily felt about that.

The truck was still gone Sunday when Tracey and Jackson took advantage of a beautiful fall afternoon and went fishing near Lake Texoma. "Mom, I bet there's a fish down there who likes gum as much as I do," Jackson said as he took his bubble gum out of his mouth and put it on the hook.

She adjusted her straw hat, reeled in her line, and then threw it back out in a different spot. Who would have ever dreamed that former fashion plate Tracey Walker would be sitting in the grass in a pair of faded jeans and an old, faded T-shirt from the Oklahoma City Zoo, with a fishing pole in her hand? Just thinking about the gasps that would bring from her high school girlfriends caused a smile to spread across her face.

Jackson sat patiently, watching his bobber, and then asked, "Mom, I'm hot. Do we have any orange juice?"

"We sure do. Bet you're glad you didn't wear jeans today." She opened the cooler and found his juice.

"Yep, I am." He took the top off and guzzled half the bottle. "Emily says her daddy wears shorts sometimes, so I guess it's all right for men to wear them, but not to school. I bet that fish who likes bubble gum is taking a nap. When he wakes up, he's goin' to be so happy because that old hook will be right in front of him with a big piece of pink gum stuck on it." He was quiet again for a minute, then he cocked his head to one side, a gesture just like Austin. "Emily says her mom gave her to her dad because he could take care of her better. She doesn't ever see her mom."

"Is that right?" Tracey asked. "Maybe her mama loved her so much that she wanted her to have the best place to live."

"Well, I'm glad you didn't give me to my dad. I would miss you much too much." He set down his rod and reel, wrapped his arms around her neck, and squeezed hard.

Tears came to her eyes. "Well, thank you very much, Jackson Walker," she said. "I shall cherish that hug forever and ever. I'd begun to think you were too big for hugs since you call me Mom and not Mommy anymore."

He let go and picked up his fishing gear again, keeping a close check on the red-and-white bobber. "Course you're important. And I'll never be too big for hugs. I think Emily would like to have a mommy, too. She's got a granny and a grandpa, and I've got a Poppa Frank and a Molly. But…" He struggled with the thought. "I just think she'd like to have a real mommy just as much as I'd like to have a real daddy."

The only time he'd ever asked about his father, Tracey had been able to hedge around the issue. She had always thought that when the time came, she would tell him just enough to satisfy his curiosity for that day. Then later, when he was older, she would tell him more.

"Do you think the fish will wake up and smell my gum pretty soon?" he asked. "I don't want to put it back in my mouth after it's been down there in that green, slimy stuff."

"I bet his nap time is just about over." She sent up a silent prayer that a fish, even a tiny perch, would swallow that hook and gum.

"Who is my daddy?" Jackson asked right out of the blue.

"Your daddy? Um—" She frantically tried to collect her thoughts into a truthful answer he would understand.

"He does have a name, don't he?" he pushed.

"Yes," she answered and realized he wasn't watching the bobber anymore.

Jackson was looking her right in the eyes without even blinking. "What is my daddy's name? Emily knows that her mama's name is Crystal. I want to know my daddy's name."

"I think maybe we better talk about this awhile before I tell you his name," Tracey said.

"Okay, what do you want to talk about? Is my daddy dead or something? I would be real sad if my daddy is dead." Jackson's voice quivered.

"No, your daddy is very much alive. A long time ago when I was in college..." she began.

"Is this a once-upon-a-time story?" he asked.

"I don't think so," she said. "I was in college and I met this man who was very special. He used to tell me he loved me Red River deep and I would say, 'No, that's not enough. I want you to love me deep as the Red River and high as the mountains,' and he would just laugh. Then he'd say he hadn't seen any mountains as high as he loved me, but he had seen the Red River during flood season, and he figured he loved me Red River deep."

"My daddy must've loved you a lot," Jackson said, "but I don't need a story. I just want to know his name."

"Story first." She wondered if it was really for Jackson or if it was to calm her own nerves. "Then one Christmas we had a big fight. I wanted him to give up a job he needed very badly and go home to Poppa Frank's with me instead, and he wouldn't do it."

"But why did he need the job so much? Didn't he have a lot of money like Poppa Frank?" he asked.

"No, he didn't. He had to work so he would have money to go to school," she answered. That part of the story was easy enough, but how did she explain the other complications to a six-year-old child? "So I went home angry and he went home angry, and we didn't talk for a whole month. When he called me, it was to tell me he was going to marry another girl, and he did. Then I had you and we've lived happy ever after."

"It was a fairy tale." Jackson sighed. "If you know all that, then you have to know his name."

"That's not important right now," she said.

"It is to me. I've got a daddy somewhere and I don't even know his name. My last name is the same as yours. Why is that?" Jackson pressured.

"Because your daddy didn't know about you," she answered. "I never did tell him because he married someone else and I..." She couldn't find the words to finish.

"Well, tell me his name and we'll go find him and tell him about me. And if we can't find him, I bet Poppa Frank will help us," he said. "My Poppa Frank can find anyone."

"I never was married to your daddy, Jackson," Tracey told him.

"Is he a mean man, and that's why you don't want to tell me?" Jackson didn't take his eyes off her face.

"No, sweetie, he is not a mean man, and he does have a name," Tracey finally answered. "And I saw him a few weeks ago and we talked about you."

"You did?" The excitement was evident in his voice. "Then he knows about me. But you didn't tell me about him. Where is my daddy, Mom? I want to see him and talk to him. I want to tell him that Poppa Frank might buy me a pony, and I want to tell him about my friend Emily and her pony, Maybelle," he rattled on.

"Do you remember when Emily said her middle name was

Trace, and I told her that's what her daddy used to call me a long time ago?" she asked.

"Yep, and my middle name is Nelson, just like Emily's daddy," he nodded. "That's funny, Mom. She's got your name and I got her daddy's name."

"Well, when Emily was a little baby, her mother decided to marry someone else. She gave Emily to Austin since he is her daddy and he got to name her all by himself."

"I know that." Jackson's tone said that he was getting more exasperated by the moment and that he wasn't going to stop asking questions until she told him what he wanted to know. "He named her Emily after his grandma who is dead now and Trace after a lady he loved a long time ago. Emily told me that."

"He named her Trace after me. I was that lady he loved a long time ago," she said.

"Oh."

"And I named you Jackson after Poppa Frank. Your middle name, Nelson, is from a man I loved a long time ago, who is your daddy," she said.

"Then my daddy's middle name is Nelson just like mine and Emily's daddy, huh?" He cocked his head to one side.

"Yes, it is," she told him. "Because Emily's daddy is your daddy, too." She said the words she'd dreaded for six years.

"Hot damn!" Jackson jumped up and hugged her tightly again. "He's the best daddy in the whole world! Emily says he is, and I believe her. Now he's my daddy, too! Can we go home and tell him? Hey, does that make Emily my cousin? She's got lots of cousins in Tom Bean. Does that make me kin to them, too?"

"That makes Emily your half sister since she doesn't have the same mother you have," she explained. "And all the Tom Bean cousins are your kin. They're your daddy's brothers' kids."

He hopped around so excitedly he didn't even see his bobber go under and wouldn't have noticed the rod and reel being pulled out to the edge of the water if Tracey hadn't grabbed it. "We got a big one," she hollered at him just about the time the line broke and the bobber floated away to the middle of the lake. "But he's gone now. He broke our line. I guess fish do like pink bubble gum."

"I got a dad-dy," Jackson singsonged. "Let's go home and see if they're back from Tom Bean yet. Emily said they were goin' down there for the whole weekend and she was goin' to ride Maybelle, but they might come home early. Can we go now? I'll help you get the stuff together." He was already reeling in the line on her fishing rod.

"Jackson, I think maybe Austin better tell Emily before

we talk to him." She took him by the shoulders and tried to explain. "You know, she might not be as excited about this as you are. After all, you'll have a daddy, but she still won't have a mommy."

He fidgeted on the drive back to their apartment. "Do you think I could call him when we get home and ask him some stuff?" he finally asked.

"What do you need to know? Just ask me," she answered.

"I just want to know that he's okay with me being his son, and you can't answer that, Mom," he answered.

"You've talked to Austin lots of times. You'll see him again soon enough."

"Well, he wasn't my daddy until right now," he argued. "I want to see him today."

"Okay, but I need to go talk to him first," she agreed.

"I'll stay in the car while you do," Jackson said.

"No, you won't," Tracey said. "You will help me take this stuff up the stairs and let me talk to him in private."

Austin's black pickup truck was parked in front of his apartment when she drove into the courtyard. She parked the Camaro and lugged the cooler and fishing gear up the stairs. Jackson carried their hats and his tackle box and followed behind her.

She dropped it all in a pile on the dining room floor and picked up the phone.

"Are you calling him right now?" Jackson asked.

Tracey nodded. "Go wash up, comb your hair, and put on a fresh pair of shorts," she told him.

"Okay." He ran off to his room.

"Hello?" Austin's voice still made her heart skip a beat.

"This is Tracey," she said.

"I'm glad you called. Listen, Emily and I started talking about Jackson, and before I knew it, she was asking why he didn't have a daddy, and anyway I ended up telling her that he did. And that I was his daddy. I know we were going to tell them at the same time, and now I've put pressure on you. If you don't tell him tonight, then she'll tell him tomorrow at school. I'm really sorry, Trace."

She sighed heavily. "I was calling to apologize to you for the same thing. We went fishing and he asked me point-blank what his daddy's name was. I tried beating around the bush, but it didn't work. He knows and he wants to come down there right now and talk to you."

"Send him down, then. These kids are readier than we are."

"So how did Emily take it all?"

"Pretty well. She says Jackson is the luckiest boy she knows, and he's got the bestest mother in the whole world, and she doesn't mind sharing her daddy."

"For now," Tracey said thoughtfully.

"Well, we can worry about that later. Are you coming over with Jackson?"

"We just got back from a fishing trip and I look like hell, but we'll be there in a few minutes," she answered.

"You'd look beautiful in a feed-bag dress tied in the middle with a rope." Austin's tone was warmly encouraging. "See you in a few minutes, then."

Chapter 9

JACKSON HELD HER HAND TIGHTLY AS THEY CROSSED THE courtyard and knocked on Austin's apartment door. Emily answered the door with a squeal, "Daddy, they're here. Come on in. Jackson, did you know you're my brother?" The little girl grabbed him by the hand and pulled him away from Tracey.

Austin leaned against the doorframe leading from his bedroom to the living area. "Hello. Have a seat. I'll put on a pot of coffee. You kids want some juice?"

"Yes, sir." Jackson stopped in the middle of the living room and stared intently at Austin, his eyes traveling from Austin's bare feet all the way up to his face. "You are my daddy. I think I look like you."

"Yes, I am, and I think you look like me, too." Austin squatted so his face was level with Jackson's. "Do you like that?"

He nodded eagerly. "What am I supposed to call you?"

"Don't be silly." Emily grabbed his hand again. "Call him Daddy. That's what I call him."

He looked up at Austin once more. "What am I supposed to call Emily?"

"Oh, Jackson, that's funny," she giggled. "You call me Emily just like you always did. Let's get some juice and go in my room and play Memory. Betcha I can beat you this time. I'm better at home than I am at school." She tugged at his hand, but Jackson just stood there.

"Any more questions?" Austin asked.

"Can I hug you?" Jackson asked.

Tears stung Tracey's eyes when Austin opened his arms and hugged his son for the first time. "You bet you can, Son," he said hoarsely. "I really do like hugs." He included Emily in the second hug.

She squealed and slipped out of her father's arms long before Jackson did. "Let's go play." She tugged at his hand again.

"You hug like Mom does," Jackson said, and he smiled then. "I think I like having you for a daddy. Are we goin' to live together like a family someday?"

"Well, we'll have to see about that. For right now you and

I will have to get used to being a daddy and a son, won't we?" Austin answered.

"Okay. Let's go play, Emily." He ran off to the bedroom with Emily.

Tracey plopped down on the sofa in the living room. Every nerve in her body was tingling with anxiety, and she didn't even realize how tense she had been until Jackson had asked that last question.

Austin settled into the couch cushions right beside her and took her hand in his. "I just need some support right now and simply touching you helps."

"Tough, huh?" she said.

"I wanted to grab him and hug him every day last week. I wanted to hold him and never let him go. I was afraid something awful would happen before I got to acknowledge him as mine," Austin whispered.

"Hey, Daddy!" Jackson ran out of Emily's room. "Can me and Emily have a birthday party together?"

"We'll think about it," Austin said.

Tracey felt his hand tremble and she squeezed it tightly.

"You sound just like Mom," Jackson said. "That's what she always says." He ran back to the bedroom and shouted down the hall. "Hey, Emily. They're going to think about it."

In a few seconds, they ran back to the living room together. "Can Jackson stay and play with me for a little while?" Emily asked.

"Please, Mom?" Jackson begged. "Is it all right with you, Daddy?"

"Maybe for thirty minutes," Tracey answered.

Austin's grip on her hand tightened. "It's fine with me."

"We'll get used to him calling you Daddy after a while," she said.

"You don't know how happy it makes me, Trace," he said softly. "Thank you."

She patted his hand, not wanting to talk about anything so emotional just yet. "Can you bring him home in thirty minutes? He needs to take a bath and calm down before bedtime."

Austin leaned over to take a quick peek down the hallway, then threw his arm around Tracey and drew her close for a kiss. He'd been drinking black coffee, no cream or sugar, and he tasted wonderful.

"Now what are we goin' to do about us?" he asked when he broke off the kiss.

"We'll worry about that later." She pulled out of his embrace. "See you in half an hour."

Exactly thirty minutes later her doorbell rang, but before she could reach the door from the bedroom where she was looking through an album of Jackson's baby pictures, he burst into the apartment with Emily in tow and Austin right behind them.

"Daddy, you've got to come in." He tugged at Austin's hand. "You've never seen my room, Daddy. Hey, Mom, I'm home now," he shouted. Then he looked up to see her standing in the doorway of her bedroom watching the commotion. "Daddy and Emily are going to see my room!"

He said *Daddy* so often, she was sure Austin's ears were probably hurting from listening to it. But he looked as proud and pleased as any man could.

"Well, you better take him in there before your toys run away. Since you weren't here, they told me they might run away from home and never come back," she teased.

"You're silly," he said, giggling.

"And when you get through seeing his room, you gotta see his mom's room." Emily joined in the conversation. "Jackson already let me look in the door, and it's beautiful. Someday when I'm a grown-up, I want a room just like it, Daddy."

Jackson rattled happily on.

"This is my toy box, and this is my bed. The other one

is where Mom sleeps when I'm sick. Last week there was a spider on that bed, and Mom hates spiders, but she put it in a grocery sack and took it down to the yard to let it go because I don't like her to kill them. Daddy, here's my closet and here's all my games, and my good Sunday cowboy boots that Mama says I have to save for good…"

"Can we go inside your room and see it now?" Emily asked Tracey.

"Maybe Tracey doesn't want us prowlin' around in there," Austin said.

"I don't mind," Tracey said. "If Emily wants a room just like mine, I expect you'd better look at it. Then you'll know what to get her."

"See, Daddy?" Emily was the first one through the open door. "Look at this yellow bed and her mirror—it looks like a window, but you can see yourself six times. Ain't it pretty?"

"Now, let's go back to my room." Jackson tugged at her hand.

"'Isn't' it pretty, not 'ain't,'" Austin corrected as the children ran out of the room. "The room is pretty, and there's no clothes on the floor either. My, how people change." He winked at Tracey.

Austin looked around the feminine, homey room and then

picked up a ring from a crystal dish on the dresser. "You've kept my promise ring all this time?"

"Of course I did," she answered. "I thought someday Jackson might want it, but if you want it back…"

"No, that's fine. I gave it to you, so it's yours," he answered.

Jackson poked his head in the door. "Can me and Emily play a little while before I take my bath?"

"No," Austin said. "It's Emily's bath time, too. And you two have school tomorrow, so we'd better go back to our apartment and get things ready. So good night, Son. We'll see you tomorrow."

"I now declare this is officially everyone's bedtime," Tracey said.

"Doing anything later tonight?" Austin asked mischievously. "We could ask Twyla to babysit and go out to celebrate."

"Sorry, I already have a date," Tracey answered pertly.

"Who with? If you don't mind my asking," Austin asked.

"With Eric Carle and Jackson. We're reading *The Very Hungry Caterpillar* for the umpteenth time."

"Oh. I see. Well, come here and give your daddy a big good-night hug, Jackson." He stooped down and took his little boy in his arms.

Tracey couldn't have asked for a better result, but why was she so sad?

"Okay, Daddy." Jackson stepped back from Austin. "Bye, Emily. The kids at school aren't going to believe that you're my half a sister. I bet they say we're making up a story."

"I bet they will." Emily slipped her hand in Austin's. "Daddy, will you carry me? I don't like to look down from way up here."

"Of course, darlin'." Austin picked her up.

"Good night, Trace," Austin said softly.

"Good night, Austin," she said. The phone rang shortly after Jackson had finally gone to sleep, and Tracey grabbed it from the end table on the first ring.

"I'm calling to ask you to go out to dinner with me tomorrow evening," Austin said.

"No," she said firmly. "I'm not ready to be seen going out on a date with you. You know how people talk."

"Then let's go to my place. I already asked Twyla if she could babysit. She'd be delighted to watch both kids at her sorority house. She and her girlfriends are starting to make decorations for the upcoming Halloween dance tomorrow night. Jackson and Emily can make tissue paper ghosts and pig out on candy corn."

"On a school night?" Tracey asked.

"She'll put them both down for a nap if they get tired. They'll be fine. How about it, Tracey? I really think we should celebrate," Austin begged.

"Okay, but when we get home—" she started.

"I thought I would order Italian for you, and we'd watch a movie here in my apartment," he said.

"That sounds wonderful," she said. "Six o'clock? But I'll make your favorite chili instead of you ordering out."

"That sounds good. I'll take the kids to Twyla," Austin said.

"Tell her that I'll pick them up at nine. That will still be a little late for them on a school night," Tracey told him.

"I can live with that," Austin said and ended the call.

"What have I agreed to?" Tracey groaned as she laid the phone down.

You have to spend time alone with him if you are ever going to figure out if you could make a family out of the mess you've both created. Molly's voice was loud and clear in her head.

━━━━━━━━

Austin's table was set for two when Tracey finally arrived and set down the casserole she'd brought. It wasn't anything fancy, just chili and corn bread baked together, but it had been a favorite of Austin's. She noted beer chilling in a tin pail of shaved ice and looked at the label. It was the kind she had preferred—back when.

She looked around for Austin and heard water running in the bathroom. He'd picked Jackson up half an hour ago, and she had told him the casserole was in the oven. Austin came out of the bathroom with his face half-shaved and half-covered with foamy white shaving cream, and a small white towel slung over his shoulder. He was bare-chested and Tracey didn't know where to look first.

"Hi! I didn't hear you knock," he said.

"I let myself in," she said. "It is six o'clock, and you left the door unlocked," she told him.

"You're a little early," he said with a grin.

"Am I?" She pointed at the clock.

There was a brief and awkward pause. Austin's nearness, his seminakedness, was affecting Tracey more than she'd ever care to admit. He'd filled out through the chest and shoulders more than she remembered. A mat of curly dark hair covered his pecs and narrowed into a thin streak that disappeared into his jeans. Tracey forced her eyes up to his face. She turned away from him and fussed with the table setting so she didn't have to look at him. She moved the forks a quarter inch to the left and the knives an equal distance to the right.

"There. That's better."

Austin gestured toward the casserole with his razor. "That used to be the only thing you knew how to cook. I loved it then and still do today. Thanks for making it for me. But you didn't have to. Next time I'll do the cooking and make you shrimp scampi."

"I didn't know you'd turned into a gourmet chef," she said.

"Shrimp scampi? No big deal. Just the kind of fast and dirty cooking I do best. You peel the shrimp, sliver some garlic, melt a little butter, and poke 'em around for a couple of minutes. Then you run 'em under the broiler for a few seconds and serve with salad and rice."

"That's the way I cook it, too," she said. "After I got pregnant, I moved out of Daddy's house, gave him back his credit cards, and learned to do everything for myself."

"Good for you. I'm going to finish shaving before we eat. Help yourself to a cold beer. That is the kind you still like, right?" he asked.

"Yes, thanks for remembering," she said.

He went back in the bathroom, and Tracey listened to

him sing while he shaved. She fought the temptation to go and watch. The wry faces he'd made when performing this daily male ritual had always made her laugh. But he looked a little too delicious with no shirt, and he might prove to be a temptation that would cause trouble. Tracey picked up a beer and twisted the top off. Before she took a sip, she rolled the icy cold bottle across her forehead, but it did little to cool her down.

Austin returned, pulling on a polo shirt.

He took a bottle from the bucket and removed the lid, then held it up. "A toast. To Jackson and Emily, who are having the time of their lives over at the sorority house."

"I'll drink to that." Tracey clinked her beer bottle with his and took a sip.

"Toast number two. To us," he said.

"There isn't an us yet, Austin," she said.

Austin caught her gently around the waist with one arm. She turned within the circle of his embrace and looked up at his freshly shaven face. His dark eyes smoldered, and he leaned down to kiss her, just once, very softly. Her lips parted and he took full advantage of that to press his mouth to hers and kiss her for real.

Tracey surrendered to his embrace, letting him hold her

close, molding herself to the strong body she remembered so well and had once loved so dearly.

She summoned every ounce of resolution she had left and gently eased away from him, putting some breathing room between them.

"Trace—" His voice was low and ragged with desire.

"I can't do this," she whispered.

"But you want to. You know it and so do I."

"Austin, if anything ever happens between us—and I don't know if or when it will..." She stopped, unsure of her own feelings or even what to say. "We have to be friends first. Then parents. Then...I don't know."

"Okay." He released her.

"I know that's not really okay with you, Austin. But that's the way it has to be."

"Forever?" he asked.

"No, not forever, but for now," she said. "Now let's dig into that casserole."

———

Tracey awoke with a start and realized the telephone was ringing. She opened one eye and looked at the clock. Three o'clock in the morning. Her first thought was that something was wrong with her father. She sat straight up in bed, her heart beating so hard she could almost see it pounding under her nightshirt.

"Hello?" she said.

"Trace." Austin's voice was raspy, and his breathing was shallow.

"Austin, what's wrong?"

"I hate to wake you, but I need help," he gasped. "Called the hospital and they said for me to come there right away. I don't think I can drive."

"Give me a minute to wake Jackson. You get Emily and meet me in front of your apartment. I'll pull my car around." She grabbed her jeans and got around so fast that her head was swimming when she picked Jackson up and carried him to the car, where she propped him up in the back seat. She drove around the apartment complex and parked beside the familiar black pickup. Austin was waiting, holding a sleeping Emily in his arms. Tracey jumped out of the car and settled Emily into the back seat next to Jackson. Then she threw her arm around Austin and supported him while he collapsed into the front seat.

His face was drawn with pain and colorless. "I think it might be appendicitis." He moaned and clutched his stomach.

She kept her voice low so she wouldn't wake the children. "I'll get you to the hospital, but you better still be breathing!"

"I can still breathe," he whispered back. "I'm not gonna die. God, but it hurts so bad, Trace. If it is, and they send me in for surgery, call my mother for me. Tell her not to worry."

Tracey drove the car right up to the emergency room doors. Two green-uniformed orderlies brought out a wheelchair and put Austin in it. Emily woke up and started to cry when they whisked him through the big automatic doors and into the hospital.

"You stay with Trace now," he whispered. "She'll take care of you. I'll be fine."

By then Jackson had also awoken, demanding that someone tell him why he was sleeping in the car and why those men were taking his daddy away in a wheelchair. Tracey drove to a parking spot as fast as the speed bumps allowed and ran with both children into the ER waiting room. They were a disheveled lot, she in yesterday's faded jeans and her hair an absolute fright, both kids in their pajamas.

"Are you Mrs. Miller?" the receptionist behind the desk asked.

"Yes," she said, without thinking, near tears herself. "Can I see him?"

"Okay. For a few minutes. But the children can't go back there," she said. "I'll keep an eye on them for a little while. It's pretty quiet tonight, thank goodness."

"Thanks," Tracey said. She explained to the children that she would be back in just a few minutes and settled them next to the receptionist. The friendly woman gave them each a picture book from a nearby rack and Tracey raced to the examination room.

"Trace…" Austin managed to stretch out a hand to her when she stepped around the curtain.

"Have you seen a doctor yet?" She took his hand in hers and held it tightly.

He nodded. "And had my blood drawn by a nurse with weird blue eyes."

"You're hallucinating," Tracey said.

"She's coming back. You can see for yourself. Anyway, Doc's almost positive it's my appendix. They're setting up for an appendectomy right now. He thinks it might have ruptured because I'm so nauseated." He held her hand tightly.

A nurse holding a clipboard opened the curtain and came over to the hospital bed. "Doc's right. You're in big trouble." She beamed at him until she saw Tracey.

Tracey vaguely remembered her from the school party

after Jackson's theatrical debut. She was one of the women who had been flirting with Austin. She was short and had gorgeous black hair and eyes so strangely blue that she had to be wearing colored contacts.

"You're scheduled for surgery in the next ten minutes. I'll prep you first." She favored Tracey with a sideways look. "Is this your sister?"

"No, my fiancée," Austin replied almost inaudibly.

Tracey just stared at him, flabbergasted. If he simply wanted her to stay in the room, he didn't have to go that far.

The nurse looked visibly disappointed. "Oh. I didn't know you were engaged, Mr. Miller."

A tall, thin doctor in a white coat looked around the drawn curtain and gave Austin a thumbs-up sign. "You'll have surgery in a few minutes, and then whether it's ruptured or not will determine how long you're in here. You must be this Tracey he keeps asking for us to go find."

"I sure am," she said.

"Call Mom. She'll get Emily," Austin said as they rolled him out into the hall.

"I'll keep Emily. You just promise me you'll wake up when this is over. Anesthesia scares the hell out of me. I'll come see you tomorrow with the kids if they let me bring them. Don't worry." She kept his hand in hers until they took him through the last set of double doors. Just before she let go, she leaned down and kissed him gently on the lips, mostly for the benefit of the ER nurse who looked all too eager to prep him for surgery.

She went back to the waiting room to find the children on the floor with several books around them. They were absorbed in reading one together, and the receptionist nodded and whispered that they had kept busy.

"Well, what's going on here? Is this a pajama party?" she asked cheerfully.

"Tracey, where's my daddy? Is he sick?" Emily began to sob.

"Yes." Tracey sat on the floor between the children, picked Emily up, and wiped the tears away. "He's got the world's worst tummy ache, but the doctor's going to make him better right now. You can stay with me and Jackson, and we'll come see him tomorrow."

"My daddy will get well, won't he?" Jackson looked like his own tears might start flowing at any moment.

Tracey wasn't about to explain an appendectomy to two worried preschoolers right then and there. Tomorrow would be soon enough when all of them could admire Austin's stitches.

"Of course he will," Tracey reassured them. "We can go home now, and you can sleep some more. Then you can go to school and when the day is over, we'll get your daddy and take him home."

"But, Mommy"—Jackson reverted back to his old title for her—"I don't want my daddy to be sick."

The receptionist looked confused, but Tracey didn't have the energy to explain the whole situation to her. She was Mommy to one kid and not the other, and they both referred to Austin as Daddy, but she wasn't Mrs. Miller. Let her figure that one out, and if she could do it in less than five minutes, she got a gold star for a high IQ.

Chapter 10

TRACEY PUT THE CHILDREN TO BED IN JACKSON'S ROOM AND then sat down on the sofa and called Austin's parents' house in Tom Bean. The last time she'd punched those numbers, she'd been in Purcell, and Austin had just told her he was marrying Crystal. When she hung up the phone that time, she tried to forget both the number and Austin Miller forever, but it didn't work.

"Hello," a cheerful voice answered. How could anyone be so cheerful at five o'clock in the morning?

"Hello, this is Tracey Walker. I'm sorry to wake you. Is this Mrs. Miller?" she said.

"You didn't wake us. I was already fixin' breakfast," the woman said.

"I'm calling about Austin. He's in the hospital, and he's had surgery. The nurse called me a few minutes ago and said that he's in recovery. He wanted me to call. It was his appendix, and they got it before it ruptured. He should be coming home day after tomorrow... No, that's not right. Today is already tomorrow, so he'll come home in—in," Tracey stammered, "about twenty-four hours. That would be tomorrow sometime."

"Do we need to come right now and get Emily? Or go sit with him?" his mother asked.

"I'll keep Emily. She and Jackson go to the same school, so she can stay with us. That way she won't miss school, and Austin said to tell you not to worry," Tracey said. "But I'm the mother of a small son so I understand."

"Austin has told us about Jackson, but that's a conversation for another day. For now, we'll have some breakfast and then drive up to the hospital," Mrs. Miller said. "I can come stay with Austin when he goes home. He'll need help for a few days. Thank you for taking care of Emily."

"Two kids are easier than one," Tracey said.

"And, Trace, come see us and bring Jackson. We're all anxious to meet the new grandson," Mrs. Miller said.

"I'll do that," Tracey promised. "After Austin is up and around. I'd be happy to bring Jackson to meet you. Thank you for the invitation."

"Family don't need an invitation," Mrs. Miller said firmly. "We'll be up there as soon as we can."

"I'll take the kids to see him as soon as school is out this afternoon. By then he might be ready for two busy children."

"Our paths probably won't cross today, but we'll be seeing you soon. Bye, now." Austin's mother ended the call.

"Grandparents!" Tracey hadn't thought too much about having to share Jackson with a huge family, but it was coming, and there didn't seem to be anything to do but accept it. "I'm not good with so much change all at once," she muttered on her way to the kitchen to put on a pot of coffee.

The day crawled. Between classes, Tracey called the hospital to check on Austin twice before lunch. His parents were there the first time; two of his brothers, the second. But Austin was sleeping, and they told her he was still groggy the few times he did open his eyes. She had a meeting at noon with the English Department to discuss new textbooks, and everyone there wanted an update on Austin.

"How did the surgery go?" Dr. Benson asked. "Were they able to do laparoscopy?"

"Yes, but he won't be back in class for a week," she answered.

"Well, with these new antibiotics he won't be laid up too long. I was in the hospital for a whole week when they took my appendix out fifty years ago. Tell him I asked after him," Dr. Benson said.

"I sure will." Tracey nodded.

"Well, hello," Damian whispered just inches behind her when she got on the elevator that morning after the meeting was over. "I hear lover boy had a busted hose last night. Is there anything I can do for *you* while he's laid up?"

Tracey turned to face him. "We were having an English Department meeting. What are you even doing on this floor?" she asked.

"Nothing." Damian held up his hands like the victim of a robbery. "I just came for the latest health bulletin on poor old Austin. And to see if his fiancée needed help with anything."

"Fiancée? Me? Who told you we were engaged?" Tracey asked.

"I'm dating a certain nurse," he answered, "the one that took care of Austin last night in surgery. Seems like you and Austin have been keeping some happy news from all of us here."

"What goes on between me and Austin is none of your damn business, Damian." She stepped out of the elevator on the first floor and ran into David Robbins.

"Congratulations on your engagement." He smiled. "I just heard this morning."

You and me both, Tracey thought. She managed a polite smile at David, who she was sure meant well, and seethed to herself.

One month ago, she didn't know where Austin Nelson Miller was or even what had happened to him. Now all of a sudden, her son knew that Austin was his daddy, and everybody seemed to think that she was going to be his wife. And she had an instant big family on a ranch in Tom Bean, Texas, that she was going to have to meet and share her son with.

How did all this happen? she wondered. Then the answers came to her in a flash.

First, Austin had gotten on her father's good side, which couldn't have been that easy. And then he'd won Jackson over in a heartbeat. Now he seemed to be maneuvering her slowly but surely toward the idea of marriage, simply by casually telling whoever would listen that she was his fiancée. Her afternoon classes were finished at two o'clock. She went by her office on her way out and found a note from Twyla on her desk congratulating her on the engagement. At the bottom was a little smiley face with his mouth turned down in a frown and tears dripping down his cheeks. Out beside it, Twyla had written, *So many sad women that he is taken.*

She slipped her laptop into her briefcase and went straight to the hospital to spend an hour with Austin before she picked up the kids at school. She found a good parking spot, visited with the volunteer in the lobby, and then rode the elevator up to the floor where Austin was recovering. She eased open the door to Austin's room and peeped inside. He seemed to be sleeping peacefully but then he moaned and fluttered his eyelids, and Tracey moved quickly to his side.

"Austin," she whispered, taking his hand in hers, amazed that it was warm since he looked so pale.

"I'm so thirsty," he muttered.

She picked up his water and held the straw to his mouth. He took a few sips and hit the button on the side of his bed to roll himself up. "Trace, I'm so glad to see you. How are the kids?"

"You look like warmed-over sin on Sunday morning," she told him.

"I feel about the same way"—he managed a weak smile—"but this doesn't hurt like it did before they took me to surgery. Now I just have to get well."

"That's the spirit." A nurse rolled a computer into the

room. "I'm here to take your vitals and bring you some pain medicine." She opened a bubble with two pills and deftly popped them into his mouth without touching the pills or his lips. Then she picked up his water cup and held it for him. "You are a lucky man. The doctor says that if you'd waited another hour, the appendix would have burst." She put a digital thermometer a few inches from his forehead, and when it beeped, she entered the number into the computer. "You can have some broth and Jell-O, and if you keep that down, we might bring a bland-food supper. Blood pressure looks good. No temperature. You can possibly go home tomorrow morning, but I'll be seeing you until after midnight for vitals," she said as she rolled her computer back out of the room.

Tracey sat down in the chair beside his bed. "That was cutting it pretty close. You don't need to be a big, tough cowboy when you're sick."

"I don't remember being tough at all," he said. "If my memory is right, I was a big baby. I hope I didn't scare the children too bad."

"The kids are fine, Austin." She patted his hand. "Emily is staying with me. Your mother and I agreed it would be the easiest thing for all of us."

Before Austin could say anything else, a short man with

thinning gray hair came into the room. "Hello. I'm Dr. Emerson. I hear you are doing very well." He pulled the sheet back and Austin's gown up.

Austin gasped when the doctor placed his stethoscope on his stomach.

"Pain or cold?" Dr. Emerson asked.

"Cold," Austin answered.

"That's good." He finished what he was doing and turned to Tracey. "Are you his fiancée? Will you be taking care of him after he leaves the hospital?"

"I'll take him home and take care of him." She nodded.

Chapter 11

TRACEY LEANED ON HER CAR AND WAITED FOR THE KIDS that afternoon. She scolded herself for not lighting into Austin for telling everyone that they were engaged. He just looked so pitiful lying there that she couldn't bring herself to start an argument. She was so engrossed in her own thoughts that the bell startled her. Jackson and Emily led the pack of little kids dashing out to the playground or to their waiting parents. They reached Tracey at the same time and clung to her in fierce hugs.

"Is my daddy alive?" Jackson asked.

"He didn't die, did he?" Emily's chin quivered.

"Your daddy is going to be fine. The doctor took out his appendix, and we will take him home tomorrow," she assured them.

"Can we go see him right now?" Emily asked.

"Yes, we can"—Tracey opened the car door—"and then after we visit him for a little while, we could go get some chicken strips and mashed potatoes at KFC for supper. Does that sound good?"

"Yes!" they said in unison and got into the back seat.

She was glad that Jackson and Emily kept each other entertained as she drove less than a mile back to the hospital. But when they arrived and stepped into the elevator, the first argument began.

"Which button, Mom?" Jackson said.

"I always get to push the button," Emily told him.

"So do I." Jackson folded his arms over his chest.

Emily narrowed her eyes at Jackson. "He was my daddy before he was your daddy, so I get to push the button."

"I just didn't know he was my daddy," Jackson argued.

Tracey hit the button for his floor. "He was my boyfriend before he was daddy to either of you, so there."

Boyfriend in the past. Fiancée today. Molly's voice in her head sounded so real that Tracey glanced over her shoulder. *Ever think that he told the nurse that so you could stay in the emergency room with him?*

"I heard my teacher say to the helper that you and Daddy

were 'gaged. What does 'gaged mean?" Emily asked when elevator doors opened.

"It means you'll have to ask your daddy."

———————

Austin felt better now that he had had Jell-O and broth. He had walked to the bathroom on his own, and the nurse had helped him put on the loose-fitting pajamas and T-shirt his mother and father had brought him. He had checked the time on his phone a dozen times, but finally he could hear the voices of his kids coming down the hall toward his room. When they came through the door, they stopped dead in their tracks.

Tracey left them there, crossed the room, and sat down in the chair beside his bed. "Give them a moment and let them get comfortable with all this. Jackson has never been in a hospital before," she whispered.

"Daddy, you need to shave." Emily took a couple of steps toward the bed.

"Are you still sick?" Jackson asked, but hung back. "Mom makes me stay in bed when I'm sick."

"I haven't felt like shaving, but I will when I get home tomorrow," Austin said. "And, Jackson, I have to stay in bed until I go home, and even then, I'll have to rest for a few days. But I can do that in my recliner. I won't have to stay in bed."

"Does it hurt?" Jackson crossed the room ahead of Emily and took Austin's hand in his. "What's that stuff hanging up there? Do you take it home with you?"

"It's the medicine they are putting in me to make me all better." He held up his arm and showed them the IV. "The medicine goes from that bag up there into my vein and..."

"And it makes you well, like the pink medicine Mom gives me when I have a tummy ache, right?" Jackson asked.

"That's right, only instead of it going in my mouth, it goes into my body."

"That's a good thing." Emily finally made her way to the other side of the bed and laid her hand on his. "I wouldn't want to have to drink that much pink medicine, but do you have to take it home with you?"

"No, I'll leave this here, but I will have to take some pills," he explained. Then he locked gazes with Tracey. "Thank you," he mouthed.

"Welcome," she whispered.

"Mom says that we get KFC for supper," Jackson said. "What do you get? Want us to bring you some fried chicken?"

"I would love that, but the doctor says I can't have fried

chicken for a few days." Austin wanted to pull both kids up on the bed with him and give them hugs, but he knew better.

"Daddy, guess what? Our teacher said that she knew you and Tracey were 'gaged and that if you got married that would make you Jackson's daddy for real. What does 'gaged mean?" Emily asked.

Jackson let go of Austin's hand and went over to the window. Evidently, he didn't care what *engaged* meant because he seemed preoccupied with pigeons or something outside.

Suddenly Austin remembered telling the nurse and the doctor that Tracey was his fiancée. At the time he just wanted to be sure that Tracey could be in the ER room with him, but evidently the news had spread.

"'Engaged' means…" He searched for an answer.

Then Jackson butted in. "Emily, come here. We're way up in the sky, and the birds are real little down there."

"I'm not looking down there. I hate to be up high," Emily declared.

"Don't be silly." Jackson turned away from the window and came back over to the edge of the bed. "Guess what, Daddy? You've got to get well fast. My birthday is only five days away, and we can't have a party in the hospital. And me and Emily want to have our party together, so you have to get well."

"I will, Son." Austin was glad that he didn't have to explain what *engaged* meant to Emily. From the glare he got from Tracey, it looked like she was the one he'd have to explain things to. He ruffled Jackson's hair and gave him a reassuring hug.

"I'm going to get out of here as soon as I can. I hope the two of you haven't been driving your mother"—he stammered—"I mean Tracey, crazy with questions."

"They've been really good," Tracey answered.

"Daddy, can me and Emily get our papers out of our backpacks and show you what we did in school today?" Jackson asked.

"I'd like that very much," Austin answered.

When Jackson and Emily took their backpacks across the room, Austin turned to focus on Tracey. "What's the matter? Don't tell me nothing. I know you, Tracey."

"Everyone thinks we're engaged, Austin. People have been congratulating me all day. I feel kind of silly saying thank you to something that isn't right."

"Who cares what people think?" he said. "I only said that because I wanted you to stay with me in the ER."

"You don't get it, do you, Austin?"

"Get what?" he asked.

"You said that we were engaged. But you never asked me." She paused to take a breath. "Everything is going at warp speed, and dealing with all of it gives me a headache. You scared the hell out of me last night, and then I couldn't stay here all night. The kids needed to be taken home, and…"

He reached through the bars of the bed rail and took her hand in his. "Will you marry me, Tracey?"

"Don't tease about something that serious," she told him.

"Who says I'm teasing? If that's what's bothering you, we can fix it right now. I've told you that I love you already. I'm not asking you to move in with me and Emily or to set a date, but I'm asking you to marry me sometime in the future," he said.

"I found mine first!" Emily shouted.

"But I've got two and you've only got one," Jackson said.

"Maybe you'd better think about that proposal for a few weeks," Tracey told him.

"That's fair enough, but until then, can we just let everyone at school continue to think we're engaged?" he asked.

"Why would we do that?"

"It would be easier than breaking up…again," Austin answered.

Tracey nodded. "That sounds like a plan. You do tend to get into trouble when we break up."

━━━━━━━━━

That night Tracey found out that getting two kids ready for bed was twice the trouble. When they gave her good-night hugs and kisses, she figured that it was also twice the joy. When she was sure they were asleep, she called Austin.

He picked up on the second ring. "I've walked the halls. I didn't need a pain pill when I could have had one. I'm so ready to come home in the morning. Mama said she would come drive me home and stay with me a few days, but..." He let the sentence hang.

"Tomorrow is Saturday. I'll come get you and help out over the weekend," she said. "Jackson is going to insist on being over there anyway."

"Thank you," Austin said. "As soon as they release me, I'll give you a call. And, Trace, thanks for everything you've already done."

"No problem," she said. "It's what a fake fiancée and the mother of your son does."

"I owe you for both," he said.

"Yep, you do, and I will collect," she told him.

"You sure didn't lose any of your sass when you became a mother," he joked.

Tracey could visualize him giving her one of his sexy winks, and just the picture in her head made her all warm and fuzzy inside.

"You still there?" Austin asked.

"Yes, I'm here, and if you want a sweet little wife who will walk two steps behind you, you might rethink that fake proposal. I'm me. Take me or leave me, but don't try to change me," she said.

"Honey, I wouldn't change a thing about you. I still love you Red River deep," he said, chuckling.

"I've decided that can be a good thing when the river is up, but maybe not so good when you could wade across it from Oklahoma to Texas." She stretched out on the sofa and used the arm for a pillow.

"But think of it this way. When it's flooding over the banks is like the good times. When it's shallow, it could be like the tough times, but the Red River never quits flowing, just like my love for you never stopped," Austin argued.

"You always were a charmer." She covered a yawn with her hand.

"And you are sleepy. I heard that yawn," Austin said.

"Good night, darlin'. I'm looking forward to the weekend, even under the circumstances."

"Good night, Austin," she said and ended the call.

The alarm on her phone awoke her at six o'clock the next morning, and for a minute she was totally disoriented. Why was she on the sofa instead of in her bed, and why was she still dressed in what she'd worn to school the day before? She sat up so fast that it made her dizzy for a few seconds, then what had happened the whole week rushed into her mind. She rolled the kinks out of her neck and went straight to the kitchen to put on a pot of coffee.

Jackson came out of his room and followed her. "Mommy, is my daddy still all right this morning? Can me and Emily go with you to get him? I'll even let Emily push the elevator button."

"You can do it." Emily rubbed her eyes as she pulled out a kitchen chair, sat down, and laid her head on the table. "If we can go bring my daddy home, I'll let you push the button."

"Of course you can both go." Tracey finished with the coffee and poured two glasses of orange juice for the kids. "How about pancakes for breakfast?"

"Yes, thank you." Emily yawned. "I love pancakes."

"Can we go right after breakfast?" Jackson asked.

"He has to wait for the doctor to tell him he can leave," Tracey answered.

"Can we please, please go wait with him?" Emily raised her head and her little chin quivered.

"I suppose we could do that," Tracey said. "He might like to have company."

"Yay!" Jackson pumped his fist in the air.

Breakfast was finished as usual by seven. Tracey took a shower, washed her hair, dried it, and was dressed by eight. The kids had dressed themselves in jeans, T-shirts that were the same color, and boots when she came out of her bedroom. A single tote bag that Emily had filled with her toys and two changes of clothing from Austin's apartment was on the sofa between them. Thank goodness Emily had a key to the apartment in an inside pocket of her backpack or Tracey would have had to go back to the hospital to get Austin's.

"I said that if we could use my tote bag to take our video games to the hospital, then Jackson could push the button," Emily explained.

"I didn't want to put my boy stuff in a bag with flowers on it," Jackson admitted, "but I like to push the button."

"I'm glad you kids are sharing." Tracey picked up her purse. "Are we ready to go, then?"

Emily shook her head. "If I close my eyes, I can come up those stairs, but it scares me to look down."

"My mom can carry you"—Jackson picked up the tote bag—"and I'll carry this. Boys ain't afraid of tall spaces like girls."

"Come here, sweetheart." Tracey opened her arms. "Why didn't you tell me yesterday morning that you were afraid?"

"I didn't want you to not like me." Emily wrapped her arms around Tracey and gave a little hop when Tracey picked her up.

"I could never not like you," Tracey assured her as she slung her purse over her shoulder and locked the door when they went outside. "You are Jackson's sister, and that makes me love you."

"I'm going to close my eyes now," Emily said. "Tell me when we are at the bottom."

At the hospital, Tracey parked beside a vehicle that looked familiar, but there had to be dozens of cars that looked like her father's in the area. Just as they promised, Jackson got to push the elevator button, and Emily carried in the tote bag. Tracey expected to see Austin sitting up in bed, but what surprised her was her father in a chair right beside the bed.

"Poppa Frank!" Jackson squealed and ran over to hop into his grandfather's arms.

"Surprise." Frank smiled at Tracey. "I was on my way to a meeting in Sherman and had a couple of hours to spare. Thought I'd stop by and check on Austin and see you."

"Well, you certainly surprised me," Tracey said.

Emily set her bag on the sofa and went to Austin's side. "Are you still coming home with us, Daddy?"

"Of course I am, but not for a couple of hours," he said. "We have to wait on one last blood test to get done."

"Emily, come over here and see my Poppa Frank." Jackson left his grandfather's side and rounded the end of the bed. He took Emily's hand in his and led her over to stand beside Frank.

"This is my friend and my sister, Emily. And this is my Poppa Frank," Jackson said. "Did I do that right, Mama? We been practicing introducing people at school."

"You did it perfect." Tracey was so glad that he'd gone back to calling her Mama instead of Mommy that she could have shouted.

"I'm pleased to meet you, sir," Emily said.

"I'm even more pleased to meet you. My little red-haired girl has grown up, so I'm glad to have another one in the family. And you can call me Poppa Frank, just like Jackson does," Frank said. "I've still got an hour before I have to leave, but maybe you kids would like to go with me to the ice cream store. I've been hungry for a brownie sundae for days, and it's no fun to eat ice cream all alone."

"Daddy?" Emily asked Austin.

"Yes, you can go with Frank and Jackson," Austin said. "Tracey and I will be right here waiting for you when you get back, and then hopefully we can go home."

"You two need to talk some more," her father whispered as he gave Tracey a quick hug and then he and the kids left.

Tracey sat down in the chair Frank had vacated. "Dad says that we need to talk. What about?"

Before Austin could answer, the door swung open. Tracey expected to look up and see the nurse bringing his discharge papers, but a stranger stood there glaring at Austin.

"What the hell are you doing here, Crystal?" Icicles dripped off Austin's tone.

Crystal's smile looked forced. "Me and Bubba was just passin' through and spent last night at my folks over in Bells. Mama said you was real sick. Someone else said you almost died. Just stopped by to see if you were alive or what, and if you were dead, if I should pick up my daughter and let her live with me."

Tracey was speechless. She had known that Crystal had

red hair, but holy smoke! Her hair was cut short and the tips were dyed platinum. She had a diamond stud on each side of her nose, and a hoop on the left side of her mouth. And was that a tongue stud that flashed when she spoke? Half a dozen bracelets jangled on her arm, and huge hoop earrings brushed against her skinny shoulders. She was so thin that her jean shorts hung on her like a tow sack on a broom handle. When Crystal scratched her head, Tracey noticed a tattoo of a rose with the stem extended underneath a gold skull ring worn on her fourth finger.

She jerked a thumb toward Tracey and spoke to Austin. "Who's she?"

"This is my fiancée, Tracey Miller."

Crystal started at Tracey's sandals and moved all the way up to her head. "So this is the rich bitch that threw you over? I can't believe you are giving her a second chance. When's the big day?"

"That's none of your business, Crystal. Why are you here?" Austin said. "I'm alive. You can leave now."

"You got no reason to talk so rude," Crystal said.

"Just leave, and don't come back around me or Emily."

"Is that what you named the brat?" Crystal asked. "You really gonna marry this fancy-schmancy broad?"

"Yes, that's what I named *my* daughter," Austin said.

Tracey's hands knotted into fists. She had been in her fair share of fights when she was a kid and won most of them. She wouldn't mind stepping off the emotional roller coaster she had been on the past few weeks and showing Crystal exactly what a fancy-schmancy broad could do.

"Whether Austin marries me or not really is none of your business," Tracey said with a saccharine smile.

"Is that so?" Crystal slapped her hands on her skinny hips. "If he marries you, then you'll be around my daughter and I guess that does make it my business."

"Emily is not your daughter," Austin said between clenched teeth. "You gave her up at birth and you've never come near her since."

Crystal shrugged. "Don't worry. I never gave a damn about the brat. I never wanted to have her at all. You know that. I just didn't want to get stuck with her now in case you couldn't take care of her because you were dyin' or something. But I'd put her right into foster care if you did die. Bubba won't raise some other man's kid. You and this bitch can have her if you want her."

"Get out! Now!" Tracey got up and went to the door.

"Don't you tell me what to do. You got no call to be so

uppity." Crystal crossed the room and got up in Tracey's space so close that Tracey could smell whiskey on her breath.

"If you want a fight, Crystal, then you'd better sharpen your claws because he sure as hell doesn't belong to *you*," Tracey said in a low voice.

"I could have him if I wanted him, and, honey, I could whip your ass from here to California." Crystal put her hands on Tracey's shoulders and pushed.

Tracey didn't budge one inch but instead drew back her hand and slapped Crystal so hard that the woman staggered against the door. If she hadn't grabbed the doorknob, she would have landed flat on the floor. Crystal bounced up on her legs like a banty rooster and drew back her fist to retaliate, but Tracey grabbed her wrist between the bracelets and the tattoo.

"Don't you worry about raising Emily," she whispered. "There's no way I'd ever let you even visit that child. You didn't deserve to have her in the first place. Get on back to that truck you live in and drive it out of town and leave us alone." She shoved Crystal out into the hall and closed the door behind her.

"I'm sorry, Trace," Austin said. "That was…"

Tracey went back to her chair. "Thank God you got sole

custody of Emily. I couldn't bear to have her living with that woman."

He nodded his agreement. "And thank God Crystal doesn't even know what she looks like, unless her parents have gotten a glimpse of her in a store or something like that."

"Do you think that she'll stay away from us?" Tracey's hand still burned, and they were both shaking.

"Us?" Austin asked. "As in you and me and Jackson and Emily."

"Yes, that's right," Tracey answered. "Austin…"

"Were you going to say something?" he asked.

"Yes, now that my nemesis is gone. God, slapping her felt so good." She chuckled and then hesitated. "And I think I love you."

"You *think* you love me?" he asked. "What does that mean exactly, and did that little catfight with Crystal help you come to that conclusion?"

"Crystal has nothing to do with this," Tracey said. "But I don't want to be rushed, manipulated, or seduced into making up my mind about anything. Is that clear?"

Austin raised an eyebrow. "Perfectly. I agree to those terms on one condition."

"What is it?" she asked.

"You take out the no-seduction clause."

"We'll talk about that another day," she answered. "You're not going to be ready for seducing me for a while anyway."

The door swung open immediately, but it wasn't the nurse. The biggest, burliest man Tracey had ever seen walked in. He wore his jeans low on his hips, topped by a gray muscle shirt with a cartoon wolf astride a Harley-Davidson printed on it. A long length of heavy chain was hooked to his belt loop, with its other end fastened to the huge billfold in his hip pocket. His dirty-blond hair was pulled straight back into a ponytail, and a full beard covered his square face.

"Hear you insulted my wife," he growled.

Tracey crossed the room to him until her nose was just inches from his. He looked strong enough to break her in half with just one swipe of his big hand, but he would have to go through her if he intended to hurt Austin.

"Yes, I did," she said.

Bubba chuckled and the tension eased. "Girl, I bet you would fight a forest fire with a cup of water."

"I wouldn't need a cup full," Tracey said. "I could put one out by spitting on it."

"Then I ain't tanglin' with you," Bubba said. He turned around and walked out of the room.

"Is this ever going to end?" Austin asked.

"I think Crystal met her match and he just came to make sure." Tracey returned to her chair once again, but her heart was pumping double time and her hands were sweaty.

Chapter 12

"YOU READY TO GET OUT OF THIS JOINT?" THE NURSE CAME in with a stack of papers and a wheelchair.

"You can't imagine how ready I am," he said.

"Get your tote bag, Emily, and you kids tell Poppa Frank—"

"They already told me thank you, and I should be going, too," her father said. "I'll call and check on y'all when I get home this evening. Bye, everyone." Emily and Jackson rushed across the floor to give him one more hug, and Tracey walked him out the door while Austin signed all the papers.

"Did y'all have time for a talk?" her dad asked.

"A little bit, but..." Tracey paused. "I'll tell you about it later tonight."

"I'll look forward to it." Frank kissed her on the forehead.

When Tracey came back in the room, the nurse was going

over the highlights of the doctor's orders. "You'll make an appointment with your primary-care physician in a week to get those stitches out. You should refrain from"—she glanced over at the children—"from extracurricular activities until the stitches are out. Take your antibiotics, and your pain pills as needed. Showers are okay, but no soaking in a bathtub. Any questions?"

"No," Austin answered. "I think that about covers everything."

"Good." She turned to Tracey. "I'm putting all these orders in your hands. You'll see to it that he follows them?"

"Yes, ma'am, I will," Tracey promised.

"So, when are you two getting married?" the nurse asked.

"We haven't set the date yet, have we, darlin'?" Austin winked at Tracey. "But we're thinking about a simple little wedding during the fall, aren't we, sweetheart?"

Tracey took a breath to steady herself. "Sure," she answered. "A beautiful fall wedding, and I'm looking at a camouflage satin dress."

The nurse laughed out loud. "Mr. Miller, I believe you've met your match."

"Yes, ma'am." Austin eased out of bed and sat down in the wheelchair. "I sure have."

Austin managed to get into the passenger seat of Tracey's low-slung sports car and remembered the time he and Tracey had had that horrible fight that broke them up.

When they reached the apartment complex, he found that getting out of the car was even tougher than getting in. By the time that he had practically unfolded himself and shuffled to the door, he wished for that wheelchair from the hospital. Once inside his place, he eased down into his recliner.

"I think I'm ready for one of those pain pills they sent home with me," he said.

"Daddy, you're okay, aren't you?" Emily kissed him on the forehead. "Do I need to call Granny?"

"No, baby girl, I'll be fine. I've got all of you to take care of me," Austin assured her.

"I'll take good care of you, Daddy," Jackson said. "You just tell me what to get for you, and I'll do it."

"Well, I could use a hug from each of you. A nice, easy one," Austin said. "I think that might make me get well real quick."

Jackson hugged him gently. "I was afraid you'd die, and I would've had a daddy for only a little while," he told Austin. "Mama said they had to poke holes in you. Can I see?"

"Maybe a little later after I get my pain medicine," he answered.

Emily kissed him on the forehead and hugged him next. "I don't want to see it, Daddy. Did it get blood on you? Does it hurt bad?"

"Yes, it does, but now my insides can get well and there's no blood." He changed the subject. "Trace tells me you two have been really good. I'm very proud of you."

"Can we go out in the courtyard and swing?" Emily asked.

Tracey looked at Austin and he raised an eyebrow.

"If you'll stay right at the swings and not wander off," Tracey answered.

"We'll leave the door open so we can hear you," Austin said.

"Come on, Jackson!" Emily grabbed his hand, and just like always, they ran to the swing set together.

Tracey sat down on the sofa. "I went over the doctor's orders, and you can have whatever you want to eat, but nothing overly spicy for a few days. Got any suggestions for lunch and supper?"

"Order out pizza for dinner, and you're the cook. The freezer is full of steaks, roast, and hamburger. Choose whatever you want to fix," he said. "What I really want is an hour in the bedroom with you."

"No extracurricular activities, remember?" she told him.

He laid his hand on the arm of the sofa. "Then would you just hold my hand?"

"Of course." She tucked her hand into his.

"I like to feel your skin against mine," he said. "I used to dream of someday when we would meet again, and I hoped when we did we could have a second chance. Did you ever think about me?"

"Just every day. I see you every time I look at Jackson, but we're not teenagers with our heads screwed on backwards," she answered.

"Okay," he said. "I can take it a day at a time if I can see you every day and we can make wild, passionate love every other day."

"Lord, we were always good in bed, Austin. That was never our problem," she said. "I was spoiled—there I said it—and you couldn't accept that. I'm not spoiled anymore, and I will always love you, but we've got to go slow."

"How much longer do you think I'll have to wait?" he asked.

"The doctor said—"

"Not for that. I mean to marry you." He stared right into her eyes.

"Not this year unless you want me to buy that camouflage wedding dress," she teased.

"What am I going to do with you?"

"That's up to you."

He laughed and then held a throw pillow to his side. "Don't make me laugh; it hurts."

"I'm glad!" She laughed with him. "You ought to hurt for all the trouble you've caused."

"You can tell everyone we're not engaged if you want to," he said when he finally got control.

"And have everyone feeling sorry for me and asking questions?" Tracey shook her head. "No, thank you."

"You are beginning to like the idea. Admit it," Austin said.

"I'm not admitting one thing,'" she said. "But I am going to make some noodle soup and sandwiches for lunch. The kids eat at eleven o'clock at school, so they're going to come in here starving in a few minutes."

"You are an amazing mother," Austin said.

"Thank you," she said with a smile as she pulled her hand free and headed for his kitchen.

When she had the soup dished into bowls and the grilled

cheese sandwiches almost ready to take out of the electric skillet, she called the children. She found a tray on the countertop beside the sink and put Austin's food on it and carried it to the living room.

"Thank you, Trace. This looks really good, and I mean that. I'm not joking. When I can share mealtime with you and the kids, it's wonderful," Austin said.

"You kids got your hands washed?" She called down the hall to the bathroom, where she heard the water running.

Jackson beat Emily to the table and bowed his head. "Mama, can I say grace for us?"

"Yes, you can," she answered.

He put his palms together and closed his eyes. "Thank you, God for letting my daddy live and for this food. Amen."

"Amen," Austin said around the lump in his throat.

"I'm starved to death," Emily declared.

"Me too," Jackson said. "Can we go back outside and play after we eat? What's for dessert? Can Daddy push us on the swings when he's all better? Hey, Mama, did you remember that I'm goin' to be six tomorrow?"

"And me too." Emily bit into a dill pickle. "I'll be six in two weeks, right, Daddy?"

"That's right," Austin said from the sofa. "And we'll have a little party even though I'm not up to par."

"What does that mean?" Jackson asked.

"I bet it means if he was a little kid, he wouldn't feel like riding his pony," Emily explained.

"Okay." Jackson accepted her explanation. "A little kid out on the playground had red spots all over him. He said he just had chicken pops but he wasn't outrageous anymore. What's chicken pops, anyway?"

"Good Lord!" Tracey looked closely at Jackson. He had had the vaccination for all childhood diseases when he was just a baby, but she still worried that he would fall in that whatever percent that got them anyway.

"That's just great," Austin said.

"Hasn't Emily had all her shots?" Tracey asked.

"Yes, she has, but that doesn't keep me from worrying about her. You've got enough on your plate right now," Austin said.

"They'll both be fine, so why are we even talking about this? That little boy said he wasn't outrageous—I mean contagious—anymore, didn't he, Jackson?"

Jackson nodded.

"I don't want red spots on me." Tears hung on Emily's thick eyelashes. "Trace, I'm scared. I don't want to look like that."

"It's all right." She reassured Emily with a hug. "If you get chicken pox, we'll give you lots of baths in a special soap and the red spots will all go away in a few days."

"Yeah, and we'll drape the mirrors to preserve her vanity and our sanity," Austin said.

"Will I get them, too?" Jackson asked.

"You've both had your shots so neither of you will get them. No sense worrying about something that hasn't happened yet," Tracey said.

"Mama, what are we goin' to do for my birthday?" Jackson asked. "Daddy can't go to the movies or out to eat with us."

"Maybe we'll have some pizza delivered right here to our door, and I'll make you a chocolate cake for after that, and then we'll rent a movie and watch it here." She made plans as fast as she could think.

"Will there be presents?" he asked.

"Of course," Austin called from the living room. "Granny and Grandpa Miller are coming with your uncles and aunts and cousins from Tom Bean. This apartment will be so full, we won't have room to put another person, and they're all bringing you presents."

"Are you making this up?" Tracey asked.

"I told them about Jackson's birthday when they came to the hospital yesterday, and they planned the rest. We can have pizza before they get here since they won't come till after supper, and Mama said she'd bring cupcakes for everyone," he answered. "She said to call her tomorrow and let her know if you need anything else."

"You're getting closer and closer to being left at the altar," she whispered for his ears only.

Chapter 13

TRACEY WAS IN AUSTIN'S BED, BUT WIDE-AWAKE. HE HAD insisted that he was more comfortable in his oversize recliner. He'd said that the power lift for the footrest made it was easier to get in and out of than his bed. She kept going over scenarios of meeting Austin's whole family and Jackson being introduced to them for the first time.

Her cell phone pinged, and there was a message from her father: Will Jackson be up at 7:30 a.m.? I want to tell him HB before he goes to school.

She started to write a note back to him but called instead.

"So you are still awake," her dad said. "I figured if you were asleep that you'd see my text in the morning and call me then."

"I can't sleep, Daddy," she said. "It's been quite a couple of weeks, and now chicken pox has shown up in Emily and Jackson's classroom."

"You had the vaccine for that when you were a kid. I remember Jackson getting it years ago. Why would any child have it now?"

"Some parents are against giving their kids the shots," Tracey said. "That's their right for sure, but I just hope these two don't come down with it."

"Has Emily been vaccinated?" Frank asked.

"Yes, so fingers crossed," she answered.

"How's Austin?" Frank asked.

"I'm at his place tonight. He's sleeping in the recliner because it's easier..."

"Hey," Frank interrupted her. "You are two consenting adults who seem to have weathered a lot of problems. I wouldn't judge if you were sharing a bed. I might not agree to it in front of the kids, but even that is your decision. But on another note, what happened in that hospital room this morning? You looked like you could spit up nails—"

It was her turn to butt in. "And spit out staples."

"That's right," he said. "Want to talk about it?"

"Crystal, Emily's mother, came to the hospital." She went

on to tell him what had happened, ending with "It wasn't very ladylike of me to slap her, was it?"

"You don't mess with a mama bear's cubs." Frank chuckled.

"But Emily isn't my cub." Tracey sighed.

"Maybe not by birth, but that little girl kind of sneaks right into your heart," Frank said. "It's getting late, and you need to get some rest. I'll call Jackson in the morning at seven thirty, and, Tracey, don't worry about his family. They'll love you just like I do." He ended the call before she could disagree with him.

She counted sheep. She counted dollar bills. She even visualized Scott Eastwood in tight blue jeans, but somehow, he kept turning into Austin. Finally, she went to sleep sometime after midnight, only to dream of dozens of children, all covered with chicken pox.

She could have slept in late that morning, but she'd set her alarm for seven and was in the kitchen making coffee when Jackson and Emily showed up, rubbing their eyes and yawning.

"Is Daddy all right?" Emily whispered.

"He's fine," Tracey said. "He'll just need lots of rest this next week."

"Are you sure?" Jackson stared at Austin, who was stretched out in his recliner. "Is he breathing?"

"I checked him when I first got up," Tracey assured him, "and he's breathing. How about some juice to start the day?"

"Yes, please," Emily said.

"And can we have bacon and eggs?" Jackson asked.

"Me too," Austin said from the other side of the living room/dining room combination. "I would love bacon and eggs, and maybe some biscuits."

"Daddy!" Emily squealed and ran over to his side to give him a hug. "You really are going to be all right, aren't you?"

"Of course I am," Austin said. "Having you kids here to take care of me will make me well really quick."

"Mama, are we going to stay here tonight?" Jackson whispered.

"Maybe," Tracey said, "if Austin still needs us. Why are you asking?"

"Daddy needs us, but I think Woof-Woof is lonely," Jackson answered.

"Woof-Woof can come see me, too. He might even help me get better," Austin said from across the room. "Emily sleeps with Lucky Jack, and I bet Woof-Woof sleeps with you, right?"

Jackson's smile lit up the whole room. "Yep, he does, Daddy."

Is he ever going to get tired of saying that? Tracey wondered.

Tracey's cell phone rang while she was putting the biscuits in the oven. "Hey, Jackson, I think that phone call might be for you. Would you answer it, please? Phone is on the table."

"It's Poppa Frank. We're doing FaceTime," Jackson said and hit the accept button at the bottom of the screen. "Hello, Poppa Frank. Are you coming to see us again today?"

"No, I can't do that; I'm at the airport about to fly out to Chicago. But I wanted to tell you happy birthday," Frank said.

"Thanks, Poppa Frank," Jackson said.

"Who all is there?" Frank asked.

"Me and Emily and Mama and Daddy. I forgot today was my birthday, and guess what, Poppa Frank, there's going to be a party tonight, and my new grandma is bringing cupcakes. I wish you were here, too. I'm kinda scared to meet all the new people. What if they don't like me?"

"Don't be scared," Frank said. "Those folks are going to like having a new little boy in their family, just as much as I like having a new little girl in our family."

"I hope so." Jackson sighed.

"Since I can't be there, I thought we'd talk about your birthday present," Frank said.

Tracey could hear as much excitement in her father's voice as she expected would soon be in Jackson's. She glanced across the room and locked eyes with Austin, who was already smiling, and one eyelid slid shut in a wink.

"Did you…" Jackson held his breath.

"I did," Frank said, "and he's going out to the ranch to live with Maybelle today. When Austin gets better, he can teach you to ride. His name is Buck on his papers, just like we talked about."

Jackson stared at the phone for a full minute, and then he whispered, "Poppa Frank, am I dreaming?"

Emily raced across the room and pinched him on the bare leg.

"Ouch! Why'd you do that?" Jackson asked.

"He ain't dreamin', Poppa Frank. I pinched him and he yelled," Emily said.

Frank chuckled. "Well, that should prove that he's awake."

"Poppa Frank, you're not just teasing me, are you?" Jackson asked.

"No, son, I'm not. Buck has been trained on a ranch with kids, so he'll be gentle and easy for you to ride," Frank answered.

Jackson laid the phone on the table and squealed. Tracey

grabbed it and turned it so that her father could see Jackson and Emily both doing a happy dance right there in the middle of the living room floor. Austin waved from his recliner and yelled, "Thank you."

"How's that for happy?" Tracey asked as she flipped the phone back around so she could see her father's face.

"Reminds me of your sixteenth birthday when I gave you your red Camaro that should have been traded in years ago," Frank teased. "My plane is boarding so I have to go. Love all of you."

"Love you right back, and thanks for everything, Daddy. Safe travels." She blew him a kiss and ended the call.

The two kids finally came to the table, but they were so engrossed in talking about Buck and Maybelle that it seemed like no one was in the whole world but the two of them. Tracey crossed the room and sat down on the end of the sofa.

"How are you feeling this morning?" she asked Austin.

"Much better. I'm going to take a quick shower and shave while breakfast is cooking, and I feel like sitting at the table this morning. I can't thank you enough, Trace, for all you've done." He laid his hand on hers. "Want to make this a lifetime arrangement?"

"What exactly are you talking about?"

"You cook, I eat. Till death do us part," he answered with a grin.

"That's a little bit one-sided there. I hear you make a really good shrimp scampi. How about we share everything from horses to kitchen? Seems like we are forever tied together since Buck is going to your ranch."

"Not my ranch," Austin said. "My folks' ranch, but I like the idea of us being forever tied together."

———

Austin was completely worn-out when he finished with his shower. He had to lean on the vanity to get through a quick shave. When he stepped out, the aroma of bacon wafted down the hall. He could hear the kids still talking about their ponies and the faint sound of Tracey humming in the background. He leaned against the wall for a few seconds and wished that he could lock the apartment door and hold on to that moment forever.

He took a few more steps and finally figured out that Tracey was humming "Love Me Like You Mean It" by Kelsea Ballerini. He remembered the day that she danced around the bedroom, teasing him by doing a little strip tease as she sang the song. After the breakup, he turned off the radio every time that song started.

"Okay, kids, who wants butter on their biscuit?" Tracey asked.

"She's a really good mother," Austin muttered. *But I'm not asking her to share the rest of my life with me because I want a mother for my kids. I want her beautiful face to be the last thing I see when I close my eyes at night and the first thing I see when I open them in the morning.*

"I'd like butter on mine, but I can do it myself," he said as he came around the corner and sat down at the table. "Has someone said grace?"

"Nope, we were waiting for you." Tracey brought two cups of coffee to the table and then pulled out a chair for herself.

"Then I'll do it." Austin bowed his head and closed his eyes. "Thank you, God, for this food, for life and hope. Thank you for allowing us to sit around this table together this morning. Amen."

When he raised his head, Tracey was already putting bacon, eggs, and a biscuit on Emily's plate and then Jackson's. After that, she passed the platter and basket of bread to Austin.

"Help yourself first," he said with a smile. "I remember that song you were humming as you cooked."

A faint blush that made her freckles a little more noticeable told him that she remembered the dance, too. "I didn't even realize I was humming."

"Did you ever think of those good times?" he asked as he loaded his plate when the food came his way.

"Of course," she said with a nod. "Strawberry jam?"

"Yes, thank you," he said.

"Daddy, will you be all better by my birthday, so we can go to the ranch and see Buck and Maybelle?" Emily asked.

"I hope so, but if I'm not, your granny and grandpa can take you kids for a day, if it's all right with Trace," he said. "But this evening, they're coming here, and Granny says that she will take a little video of the two ponies and bring it for you to see. How's that?"

Emily turned her face toward Jackson. "See, I told you they would like you."

"I wish we could make this day go faster." Jackson sighed.

A loud clap of thunder made both kids jump, and then hard rain beat against the windowpane. Jackson groaned. "And now we can't even go outside and swing, and if it's rainin' at the ranch, we might not get to see Buck tonight."

"Granny will figure out a way," Emily said. "She always does."

"After breakfast you kids could watch *Home on the Range* on Emily's DVD player in her room. That would make the time go by faster," Austin suggested.

"Yes!" Jackson pumped his fist in the air. "That's my favorite movie. It's where I got the name for my pony. Buck was this horse that was an outlaw at first, but then he got good."

"Lucky Jack was a rabbit with a wooden leg," Emily said. "I felt sorry for him, so I named the bunny I sleep with after him. When I was just a little kid, I slept with another bunny, but he kind of fell apart, and Daddy got me Lucky Jack to take his place. But Fluffy is still in a box on my closet shelf."

"I just wish breakfast would be over so we could have some adult time together," Austin whispered for Tracey's ears only.

"Me too," she answered.

As soon as the kids finished breakfast, they raced off to Emily's room. Rain continued to pour like someone was spraying down the complex with a fireman's hose. Every now and then, lightning would flash through the downpour and thunder would roll overhead.

"I'm glad we didn't have to try to bring you home in this kind of weather," Tracey said.

Austin slowly got to his feet and started to help clear the table.

"You go sit down," Tracey said. "I can do this."

"I couldn't go to sleep last night so I read over the doctor's orders. I can lift anything if it weighs less than ten pounds," Austin said. "That means I can't marry you for a while, because when I do, I plan to carry you over the threshold."

"Well, then, no wedding for at least six weeks, right?" she teased.

"I might heal a lot faster if you'd give me some hope." He put the jam in the refrigerator and cornered her in the small galley-style kitchen. "Is there hope?"

She put her arms around his neck. "There is hope, Austin, but I don't want to be rushed. We still have an attraction for each other, but we're not those crazy kids anymore. We have responsibilities, and we need to figure out if there's life beyond lust."

"There is for me," he said.

"Let's be sure." She tiptoed and brushed a kiss across his lips. "Let's get over this euphoria of how well everything is going right now and settle down to the real world before we make any plans."

"That's reasonable." He tipped up her chin with his fist and really kissed her, tasting the combination of coffee and bacon on her lips.

When the kiss ended, she took a step back. "That's enough excitement for you today, and more than enough for me. We've got kids to try to entertain all day, and I do have to wrap a few gifts, so I'll have to run between the raindrops back to my place sometime before your folks arrive."

"Look!" He took her hand in his and led her to the living room and pointed out the window. The storm had passed, and a lovely rainbow looked as if it had been painted right on the window. "Is that an omen or what?"

"It just might be," she agreed.

―――――――

"The pizza deliveryman just pulled up outside," Austin called out later that afternoon.

"Thank goodness," Tracey said.

Keeping two hyper kids entertained on a birthday had just about drained her, and now she had to think about meeting Austin's parents for the first time in only an hour. She wished that she had gone home with him one of the many weekends when they were dating, or even just driven from Durant to

Tom Bean on one of the many evenings he'd begged her to go with him to the ranch. It was barely an hour's drive, but she had been as stubborn as he was back then. If he couldn't make time to go meet her father, then she wouldn't go see his parents.

"Pizza, pizza!" Both kids ran out of Emily's room where they had been playing Candy Land and hopped up into their chairs at the kitchen table. "Happy birthday to me, happy birthday to me," Jackson singsonged.

They had finished supper and Tracey had taken the pizza boxes out to the trash can when a caravan of pickup trucks pulled up in the parking area at the far end of the courtyard. Both kids had had their noses pressed against the living room window since they had swallowed their last bite of pizza.

"They're here, Jackson!" Emily squealed and pointed. She grabbed Jackson's hand and pulled him out the door.

Austin eased up out of his chair and took Tracey's hand in his. That gave her a small measure of confidence as his family paraded into the apartment. They used the coffee table to drop gifts and the kitchen table to lay out trays of cupcakes and set up a punch bowl that someone quickly filled with sherbet and ginger ale. Jackson and Emily were hopping around like the excited kids they were, going from one person to another.

"Hey, everyone, if we could all quiet down." Austin raised his voice and the buzz of a dozen conversations stopped. "I'd like to make some introductions."

Tracey's heart kicked in an extra beat, and her pulse raced. She hadn't thought about so many people being there, yet the whole family had turned out for Jackson's party.

"Folks, I want all of you to meet my Trace," Austin said. "You've heard me talk about her for years, and I'm happier than I can say to finally introduce her to you. I'm sure Emily has made all of you acquainted with Jackson. Tracey, this is my father, Andrew, and my mother, Ellie, and these are my four brothers and their wives." Each one stepped up to say a few words to her as they were named.

"It's going to be a while before I get all your names and faces right, so be patient with me," Tracey said when introductions were done. "I'm very glad to meet you, and thank you for accepting Jackson like this."

"Oh, honey, he's the spitting image of Austin at that age. We're so glad to have him in the family"—Ellie gave Tracey a side hug—"and to finally get to meet you. Welcome to our crazy family. We've got ten granddaughters, but Jackson is our first grandson. We're so looking forward to getting to know him."

"I told you it would be fine," Austin whispered.

Tracey squeezed his hand. "Jackson is going to be spoiled rotten."

"Can't help that," Austin said. "They've spoiled every one of their grandkids, but I was thinking that maybe we could give them a few more grandsons, just to even out the odds a little."

"Maybe your brothers could help with that," she said.

"Oh, no!" Austin said. "I'm the baby of the five boys, and I was one of those oops babies. My youngest brother over there talking to Jackson is fifteen years older than I am. The oldest one is twenty years older than me. They aren't having any more kids, and all ten of their daughters are either in high school or college."

"We're not rushing," Tracey reminded him.

"No, but we are sure hoping." Austin kissed her on the forehead.

Chapter 14

AUSTIN FELT A SLIGHT TWINGE OF PAIN IN HIS SIDE WHEN HE stepped up into the cab of his black pickup truck, but it felt so good to be dressed and out of the apartment, dressed in something other than sweatpants after eleven days. The stitches had come out the day before, and the doctor had released him to go back to work. But only if he took it easy and didn't lift anything for a few more weeks.

Emily and Jackson were buckled into their booster seats in the back seat. Tracey was in the front seat beside him, and if those weren't Roper boots she had on her feet, he'd eat his belt buckle for lunch and have a handful of grasshoppers for dessert.

They hadn't even gotten out of Durant when Jackson asked, "How much farther is it, Daddy?"

"We should be there in a couple of days, partner," Austin said in his best cowboy drawl, "if the dust storms don't make us stop this covered wagon. We might have to ration the water supply if that happens. I know it'd be hard on you and Emily not to have a bath for two days and not to see your horses for that long, but a covered wagon can only go so fast."

"Oh, Daddy, you're silly," Jackson said.

Then he and Emily started a conversation about their ponies and how they were going to pretend they were riding across the prairie to somewhere way off. Maybe even as far off as the galaxy. They debated whether or not the Star Wars crew kept ponies in their spaceships.

Austin reached across the console with his right hand and massaged Tracey's shoulder. "You're kinda quiet today. Are you worried about seeing my folks again?"

"No… Yes… I don't think so," she stammered.

"Which one is it?" Austin pressured.

She wouldn't answer. Austin tried a different approach. "You're looking mighty fine today." His voice dropped to a whisper. "The only way you look finer is when you're wearin' nothing at all."

"Thanks for trying to take my mind off going to the ranch. You've talked about it so much that I'm a little intimidated by just visiting it." She smiled a little. "How far is it to Tom Bean? I have to go."

"Sorry, darlin'." He went back into the slow cowboy drawl. "There's only one outhouse between here and there. Last time I checked, it didn't have any toilet paper in it, but there was a 1901 Sears catalog hanging on a wire on the inside wall. I think the rattlesnake who lives in there has probably holed up for the winter in the rocks behind it, so you don't have to worry about him. Unless he's in a bad mood," Austin drawled. "He gets a little cranky sometimes during this time of year. People from Oklahoma keep poking him and he hates that, so if you see him, you tell him that you are thinking about changing your citizenship to Texas."

Tracey smiled wider. "I didn't know you were a comedian."

"It will take a lifetime to figure out all the mysteries I've gotten hid away special for you," he said. She hadn't known Austin could be so wonderfully silly.

"Daddy, I'm thirsty. How much farther is it?" Emily piped up from the back seat.

"Just a few more miles, baby. We can stop in Denison and get something cold to drink, but no cookies or ice cream. Granny's been cookin' for three days, and if we don't do justice to her food, she'll think we don't love her." He looked back in the rearview mirror at Emily while he talked. "Okay?"

"Okay, Daddy."

"Daddy, you still haven't told me what 'gaged means," Emily said. "My teacher said you were 'gaged to Tracey. Grandpa told Uncle Boone he got a new thirty-gauge shotgun. Are you buying Tracey a shotgun?"

"No, Emily." Austin chuckled. "'Engaged' means that two people are planning to get married."

"Wow! That's awesome!" Jackson shouted. "Does that mean you two are getting married? We can all live in the same apartment!"

"Are you goin' to be my mommy, Tracey?" Emily whispered.

"Now look what you did." Tracey shot a look over at Austin.

"When? When are you goin' to marry my daddy?" Jackson's voice filled the whole truck.

"We haven't decided," Tracey answered, "but when we do, you kids will be the first to know."

"Daddy said he loves Mama. I heard him say it last night," Jackson whispered loudly to Emily.

"You can't fight it forever, Trace." Austin picked up her

hand and kissed her knuckles. "I want to spend my life with you. And raise these kids and wake up with you next to me every morning."

"I am thinking about it, but you really need to be healed up before we set a date and do all that stuff. Do we really want a big hoopla, or do we just go to the courthouse?"

"Maybe something in between," he answered. "We want our families there, so the courthouse is out, but nothing huge, unless you want the whole nine yards."

"What did you do the first time around?" she asked.

"We went to the courthouse and lived in a trailer house I had rented," he answered. "What does that have to do with us?"

"A lot," Tracey answered. "We can't run from our past. I don't want a wedding like what that woman had, so I needed to know before I go buy my camouflage wedding dress."

"She wore jeans and a T-shirt from a rock concert. I wore my jeans and a western shirt. We got married. I went back to work at the feed store, and she went to work as a waitress. She wanted to go out and get drunk that night, but I told her she couldn't drink until the baby was born. That set off our first big fight, and things went downhill from there." He lowered his voice. "I was surprised that Emily weighed eight pounds and had no signs of being a drug baby."

"Okay." Tracey nodded. "Now we don't have to ever talk about this again, and, honey, I promise I won't wear a camouflage dress."

"Or one with a thousand buttons down the back?" he asked.

"You got it," she agreed.

He pulled over at a convenience store in Denison, where everyone went inside for a bathroom break and then to get something cold to drink. Once they were back in the truck, they left the city and Austin watched the familiar sights of his part of Texas go by at seventy-five miles an hour.

"Look at all that cotton," Tracey said. "Do your folks grow any?"

"No, they're cattle ranchers," Austin answered as he turned into the lane leading up to the Miller ranch.

"We're nearly there!" Emily shouted. "I can see Maybelle in the pasture, and there's Buck right there beside her. Look, Jackson, he's got a white face and brown on his back."

"Go faster, Daddy," Jackson said. "Drive like Mama when she's going like a bat out of hell."

Emily made a whistling noise when she sucked in air through her teeth. "You said a bad word."

"Sorry," Jackson said, "but Poppa Frank says that's the way she drives."

Austin chuckled. "Sometimes a bad word just slips out."

"Yep, they sure do," Jackson agreed.

The children were unbuckled and out of the truck within seconds after Austin parked. They were little more than a flash of red and one of dark hair in a blur as they ran to the pasture fence where Andrew waited. Saddles rested on the fence. He picked up each kid for a hug, then set them down. Austin couldn't hear what he was saying, but he could imagine it was pretty much the same speech his father had given him when he got his first pony. *Before you ride, you have to get to know the animal. Talk to him and get comfortable with him.*

"Should we go out there?" Tracey asked when she was out of the truck.

"Not really. Dad is an old hand at dealing with kids, and to tell the truth, that drive tired me more than I want to admit," Austin answered.

Granny Ellie waited on the front porch. An apron was tied around her waist, and she wore faded jeans topped by a red T-shirt with the sleeves rolled up. Her blond hair was curled softly around her face, and she didn't look a day over forty.

"Come on in the house. Andrew has been waiting for an hour for those kids. I'll fix you both a glass of sweet tea," Ellie said.

"We just had a soda, but I could sip on some tea," Austin said.

"Me too," Tracey said.

The two-story white frame house had a wraparound porch and several doors on the second floor leading out to a catwalk. The front door opened into a great room that housed the living room, dining room, and kitchen all in an open floor plan, with a staircase off to the right that evidently led up to the bedrooms.

"I'll give you a tour of the place later, Tracey, so you'll know where everything is," Ellie said. "It's too big a house for two old people, but when the boys were all home, sometimes I thought it was way too small."

Austin sat down in one of two recliners. "And it's not too big when we all gather for holidays, is it?"

"On those days, it's just barely big enough," she answered.

"Does all the family come home?" Tracey followed Ellie into the kitchen.

"They all live within five miles of us," Ellie answered, "and I expect them all to be here for Thanksgiving. I'm not too picky about Christmas since I get them for Thanksgiving. That way if the other side of their families want them, I'm willing to share. If they don't have plans, they know the door is open here to celebrate with us. You and Jackson and your father are all invited anytime we have a family gathering."

"Thank you. We'll have to see how things work out," Tracey said. "Can I help you with anything?"

"Yes." Ellie nodded as she poured tea over ice. "You can take a glass in to our invalid."

"I heard that, and I'm not an invalid," Austin argued.

"How did your first time at drivin' go? Wear you out, Son?" she asked.

"A little, but it sure feels good to get out of that apartment. Thank goodness I don't have to stay cooped up for a month. I'd be crazy as a loon." He answered as he took the glass from Tracey and whispered, "I might not be nearly as crazy if I could be stranded on an island with just you and me for a whole month."

———————————

An hour later the kids burst in the back door, both talking at once.

"Whoa!" Tracey held up a hand. "One at a time."

"You go first," Emily panted.

"Grandpa says we can ride," Jackson said. "I even helped

put the saddle on my pony and Buck likes me and…" He stopped for a breath.

"And we want y'all to come watch us ride in the corral. That's all Grandpa says we can do today, but when we come for my birthday, we get to ride the fence row," Emily finished for him.

"They're almost like twins," Ellie said.

"Yep." Austin grinned as he took Tracey's hand in his and led her out the back door. "You kids lead the way, and we'll follow, but don't mount up until we're there. We promised Poppa Frank that we'd film it for him."

Jackson skipped along right ahead of Austin and Tracey. "Buck is the best pony in the whole wide—"

"World," Emily said.

"I've got my phone right here in my pocket," Ellie said.

"So do I," Tracey told her. "Dad would never forgive me if I didn't send him a video as soon as Jackson is riding."

"Put your boot in the stirrup, like this," Emily told Jackson. "Then you swing your other leg over and settle into the saddle."

Jackson did just what she said.

"Now get reins in your hands," she told him.

"Would you like me to lead him around the pasture for you once or twice?" Grandpa asked.

"Nope," Jackson said firmly. "But you forgot to tell me to lean down and kiss his mane and whisper in his ear how much I love him," he said. "That's what the cowboys do on the shows I watched about them."

"That's right, my boy, I did forget." His grandfather nodded. "That's probably the most important part of ridin' a pony."

Tracey grabbed Austin's hand and squeezed until the pony started to move at a slow pace around the corral. When Jackson didn't fall off, she loosened her grip, but he kept her hand in his.

"He's a natural," Austin said. "We've worried about him for nothing."

When Jackson turned in the saddle and waved at her, she let out a long whoosh of air, jerked her hand free, and waved back at him.

"It's all right, Trace." Austin put his arm around her waist. "He's a natural rider. Daddy said I was like that when I was about his age."

"Austin could ride anything," Andrew said. "We got him a pony when he was six, but before that he rode the sheep in the local rodeo. Won a trophy when he was five. Strapped his hand down like the bull riders, put the other one up in the air, and off they went. Jackson will be just fine, Trace. He's a Miller. Millers are born with horse sense. And besides, your daddy bought him a gentle little pony, so don't worry."

Tracey laughed. "I'm a Walker, and we were born to worry."

"He's doing good, and we've got lots of videos, so let's me and you go back to the house, Trace, and leave these guys to talk cows and plowing." Ellie looped her arm in Tracey's.

"See you later," Tracey told Austin. She'd watched Jackson ride around the pasture a couple of times without falling off and fracturing his skull or breaking an arm, but Jackson was a bit of a daredevil. "Please watch him closely. He's not afraid of anything."

Ellie opened the wooden screen door into the country kitchen. "I got a text from Austin's brothers. Looks like they're anxious to spend time with you and Jackson, so they're all coming for supper. I kind of figured that's what they'd do so I made a double batch of bread." She moved a huge bowl of yeasty-smelling dough to the cabinet, dumped it out on a floured piece of waxed paper, and began to knead it.

"I loved it when Molly made bread. That's our house-keeper and cook, but she's more than that. She's family," Tracey said.

"My boys used to love to walk in the door after school and smell homemade bread bakin'," Ellie said. "Before I get too busy with makin' dinner, I want to tell you how glad I am that you and Austin found each other again after all these years. Lord, I nearly gave up on him that Christmas six years ago. Never had any trouble with him before but all of a sudden, he was out drinkin' with that awful Crystal. Then he walked right into this kitchen and told me and his daddy he was marryin' her. We were heartbroken. We told him we thought marrying her was a mistake. That was one time I wished that we hadn't taught him to always do the right thing."

"It's all in the past," Tracey said.

"Yep, it is. Thank goodness," Ellie said. "But I want you to understand how we see the situation. Crystal just up and left him with Emily. I try to be a step-in mother when I can but it isn't easy. She's goin' to get to the point where she needs a real mother, just like Jackson needs a real daddy. I'm so glad you and Austin are engaged. You know, Austin hasn't been a whole man all these years without you. He completed his education and he's a good daddy to Emily, but that wasn't ever enough. Since you two found each other again, he's got some life back in his eyes and he jokes with us like he used to. For so many years, he's just been a shell. Then you came back in his life. I just wanted you to know that before all the relatives got here."

"Mrs. Miller..." Tracey bit back tears. "Thank you."

———————

By the time all the families had arrived, the kitchen and dining room tables were filled with food of all kinds. Tracey didn't know if she'd ever seen so much food for just one day in her entire life. Molly usually made a big spread for holidays, but this was just a Saturday family supper.

"Do you do this often?" she asked Kelly, one of the sisters-in-law.

"Oh, at least once a month, sometimes two or three times. The kids like to come and see Granny and Grandpa on weekends. Sometimes Grandpa needs to get hay in and our daughters, Tiff and Steph, can drive a tractor. Or if need be and they're not arguing, they can tear down an engine and work it over if it needs doing. Sometimes Granny needs us to help put up soup or green beans or corn when it gets ripe, so we help with that. If they don't need anything, sometimes we all gather at one of our houses to catch up on the work there. It's just a family thing, I guess. Jackson sure is a cute kid. I can see him lookin' just like Austin when he gets older. Folks always tell us Austin and my husband and his brother Dallas look a lot alike."

"Is Dallas the oldest?" Tracey asked.

"Nope, it goes like this. Think of it as reverse alphabet. Houston is the oldest, then Dallas, then Crocket, Boone, and Austin," Kelly answered. "You'll get us all straightened out before long."

Tracey was glad that Kelly had that much confidence in her, but four brothers, their spouses, and all ten of Austin's nieces—well, it wasn't damn likely but she would give it her best shot.

"Gather 'round," Ellie called out. "We're serving buffet style tonight, and you can find a chair or cop a place to sit on the floor. Andrew, darlin', you can offer up grace now." Ellie bowed her head, and everyone followed suit. Austin slipped his hand under the table and took Tracey's hand in his while his father prayed, giving thanks for the day, the food, and the newest members of the family—Jackson and Tracey.

Chapter 15

At noon on Friday of the next week, Tracey got a phone call to come pick up her son at school. He had spots on his neck and was running a slight fever.

"But it can't be chicken pox. He's had his vaccinations and all the boosters," Tracey said.

"I'm afraid several kids have come down with it even though they were vaccinated," the nurse said.

"I'll be there in a few minutes," Tracey said.

"He'll be waiting in the office," the nurse informed her. "You can put him on distance learning so he won't miss anything."

"Yes, ma'am, I will do that," Tracey said and ended the call.

She had just stepped into the elevator when Austin caught

up with her. "I got a call from school. Emily has chicken pox."

"So does Jackson. I'm going to get him right now," Tracey said. "What are we going to do?"

"Well, I called Mama, and she said to bring Emily to the ranch. I know she would love to have Jackson come, too, since they could entertain each other," Austin said.

"I can't leave him for two weeks like that." Tracey groaned. "I'd be crazy with worry, and he wouldn't be happy."

"You don't have to," Austin said. "We can commute for two weeks. There's plenty of room at the ranch house. It's less than an hour's drive up here and back in the evening. We can carpool."

"Or I could call Molly to come take care of Jackson," Tracey said.

"He'll be happier at the ranch," Austin said as the elevator doors opened. "The nurse said they could do distance learning the two weeks they're out of school. Mama is already going to help Emily, and we can take care of whatever homework they haven't gotten done in the evenings when we get home. They're going to be miserable without each other. You already know that." He took her hand in his. "We can take my truck to get them."

"All right," she agreed. "That does make more sense than having to separate them for two whole weeks, but you need to make it right with Ellie before we say anything to the kids."

Austin called his mother on the way to the school and put the phone on speaker.

"I would love that," Ellie said. "Two is less trouble at times like this than one, and I've been through this before. All four of your older brothers got it when Houston was in the first grade. He brought it home to the other boys, so I had four back then. Two will be a breeze. Do I need to get one or two rooms ready for you and Tracey?"

"Two for now," Austin said.

"Thank you for that," Tracey said when the call ended.

Just like the nurse had said, the kids were waiting in the office, and both looked miserable. Emily started to cry when she saw Tracey. "Am I going to be ugly?"

"Do they hurt?" Jackson's chin quivered.

"They itch, but if you don't scratch them, they probably won't scar." Austin dropped down on his knees and gathered them both to his chest in a hug. "And, Emily, these little bumps will go away, and you will always be beautiful."

"But, Mama, can me and Emily stay together? Can Molly come keep us both?" Jackson begged.

"How about if Granny Ellie thinks it's all right, you both go out to the ranch and stay until you are over the bumps?" Austin asked.

"I don't want to be away from Mama that long," Jackson said.

"I don't want to be away from Mama that long either," Emily declared.

Had Emily really called her "Mama"?

"Neither of you will be away from me or your daddy. We will leave you just like we do when you are in school, but we'll be right there every morning and as soon as our classes are over," Tracey assured them. "Why don't we go home and get some things packed up and ready to go?"

"Lucky Jack?" Emily whined.

"And Woof-Woof and Cowboy Bear?" Jackson asked.

"All of those, plus pajamas and then we'll stop by the drugstore and pick up some special stuff for your baths that will stop the itching," Austin said.

Tracey cut her eyes around at him.

"I just got a text from Mama listing everything to make them more comfortable." He shrugged.

"Thank God, then, for Granny Ellie." Tracey sighed.

"Mommy," Jackson asked on the way home, "can Molly send us some gravy in the mail?"

"No, honey. You can't mail gravy. Maybe she can send you some cookies, though," she said.

"I'll puke if you talk about gravy right now. I want orange Jell-O," Emily said. "Granny Ellie makes good orange Jell-O when I'm sick."

"That sounds good, too, and ice cream," Jackson said.

That started a back-seat conversation about what they wanted to eat later. Austin reached over the console and laid a hand on Tracey's shoulder. "We'll get through this, darlin'."

"Emily called me Mama," she whispered.

"Did that bother you?" he asked.

"No." Tracey shook her head. "It made me feel good."

"We're going to be a family," Austin said, "but I want you to be comfortable with the changes that will bring."

"I'll be glad to be her mama," Tracey said.

———————

The next two weeks were hectic to say the least, but Tracey and Austin got a lot of talking and a lot of issues worked out on the commutes to and from the college each day. She admitted that she had a lot of trust issues to get over. He told her that he admired her for the way she'd taken control of her life.

The day that the kids could finally leave the ranch was downright bittersweet. Ellie almost cried at the breakfast table. Jackson declared that he didn't want to leave. He liked living on the ranch and doing his schoolwork on the computer. Emily wept until her eyes were swollen and red.

"It's Friday," Ellie said that morning. "Let them have one more day away from school and run and play over the weekend."

"Please, Mama," Jackson begged.

"Will you promise to go home Sunday night and not be sad?" Tracey asked.

"I promise"—he laid a hand on his chest—"with all my heart."

"Me too," Emily said. "We want to ride Buck and Maybelle, and we haven't even got to go outside for all this time."

"Okay then, it's a deal," Austin said.

"Now, with that in mind," Ellie said. "You both have been stressed over all this, so I insist that you go out to eat somewhere tonight, and then go to a movie. You need to have a real date and relax for an evening."

Tracey started to argue, but then thought about how nice it would be to actually have a date with Austin. "Thank you, Ellie," she said.

"You are so welcome." Ellie patted her on the shoulder. "Now, you two best be getting on the road or you'll be late for your first class."

"Where are we going on this date tonight?" Tracey asked when they were in the truck.

"I thought maybe we'd go to Salita's. If I remember right, you like Mexican food better than anything...other than a back rub under your bra strap."

"Good memory," Tracey said with a smile. "I love that place. What movie are we going to see?"

"You can choose, or we can just sit in the park and talk," he said.

"I thought we'd covered most everything on our commutes," she said.

"We haven't talked about money," he said.

"That topic wouldn't last two minutes. We're professors. We don't have millions that would warrant a prenup." Tracey chuckled.

"Actually, I've saved up enough for a down payment on a few acres," Austin said. "There's a piece of land I've looked at just east of Calera. It's about fifteen minutes from the college so it's a very short commute. The children could still go to school here in Durant. There's a small three-bedroom house on the property with plenty of room to add on," he said.

"And you want to buy this land? How many acres?" she asked.

"Sixty," he said. "I could buy about a hundred more right next to it later on, if I wanted to run a few more cows. There's even a small hay barn for Buck and Maybelle to be put in during bad weather."

"And you want this land, right?" she asked.

"I won't buy it if you've got a mind to live in town," he said.

"I never did live right in town, you know," she said. "I've saved up a little, too, and I have a healthy trust fund from my mother that I've never touched. I've often thought about buying a little house for me and Jackson."

"But I want to pay—" He stopped himself.

"Pride sure can mess up a hell of a lot of lives," she reminded him. "If we pooled our money, then we might be able to buy the other hundred acres."

"Are you willin' to live in a little town?"

"If you'll let me pay for part of it. Remember what I told you about sharing?"

"O-kay." He drew out the word like he always did.

"Is that all? We have forty-two miles to go, and we used up the money discussion."

"That's all for now," he said with a wide grin. "Now all we have to do is set a wedding date, and maybe…"

"That 'maybe' could be soon." She leaned over the console and kissed him on the cheek. "I love you, Austin Walker."

"I love you, too," he whispered.

"Maybe Sunday we can drive down to Calera and look at the place," she said before she told him to pull over at the next motel.

"I can call the real estate agent tomorrow and set it up," Austin said. "He's a friend of mine and the house is already vacated. He says it needs some new carpet and a little paint, but that's about it."

"That would be nice," she said. "I'm sure you've seen the property, but I'd like to take a look at it before we make up our minds for good."

"I love you. I love you Red River deep, and I want you to be my wife more than anything in the whole wide—"

"World!" She finished the sentence for him. "Let's set the date. How about over Thanksgiving break? We could get married on Thursday evening after our big meal at your folks' house, then have a short three-day honeymoon. Either Ellie or Dad would probably be glad to babysit for us."

"Trace, you've just made me the happiest man in the whole...world," he said. "The way I ruined our chance at love, I didn't figure I'd ever get a second chance."

"Hey, you can't carry that burden alone," she told him. "My attitude in those days left a lot to be desired, too. But let's forget about the past and dwell on making a future."

"You are amazing," Austin whispered.

"And one more thing," she said. "I want to talk to a good lawyer as soon as possible. I want to adopt Emily as my own. Then when she calls me 'Mama' it will be for real."

"Tracey Walker," he said softly. "You are beyond amazing. I love you so much." Austin brought her hand to his lips and kissed her knuckles.

―――――――――

The day seemed to drag by like a slug on its last journey through life, and when the last bell rang, Tracey grabbed her briefcase and was in the elevator in seconds. When the doors opened on the ground floor, Austin was standing right there.

"Are we ready for our date?" he asked.

"I thought maybe we would have dessert first?" she said.

"Braum's for ice cream?" he asked.

"No, I was thinking your apartment for a different kind of dessert." She winked at him.

"Oh," he said with a grin. "I would like that very much."

He took her free hand in his, and they walked across the campus to his truck. He kissed her as he helped her into the passenger seat, and then he drove straight to the apartment complex. "I would like to carry you over the threshold," he said as she parked in his designated spot.

"But, darlin', I weigh a little more than ten pounds," she reminded him. "You can carry me over the threshold into our new home when we come back from our honeymoon."

Austin began with slow kisses the minute they were inside the apartment. "There's no hurry for this dessert, is there? I've waited so long for this day that I don't want to rush."

"No hurry at all." She slowly undid one button at a time on his shirt.

There was a string of clothing all the way down the hallway when he backed her into the bedroom and kicked the door shut with his bare foot.

Chapter 16

TRACEY WAS MARRYING THE ONLY MAN SHE EVER REALLY loved and the father of her child that day. When she stretched herself awake that morning in the Miller farmhouse, there was peace in her heart.

She pulled the curtain back in what had become her bedroom and looked outside. Austin and Jackson were walking across the yard together, going toward the pasture fence, but Buck and Maybelle weren't there anymore. They were already in their new barn at the house in Calera. Tracey couldn't believe so much had happened in so short a time. She and Austin and Jackson had looked at the house and land, and then little Jackson had told his Poppa Frank all about it.

The very next day, the real estate agent called to tell them that Frank Walker had paid for the parcel of land in full.

When Tracey called to tell him that wasn't the way things were going to be done, he told her flatly to shut her pretty mouth. It was his wedding gift to them, and he wasn't taking no for an answer. Besides, he reminded her quite loudly, everything he had would be hers someday and it wasn't any fun to make money if he didn't have anyone to spend it on.

The Miller family had pitched in after work and on the past four weekends to paint the outside and inside of the new house and clean out the barn for Buck and Maybelle. Just last week the new carpet had been installed, and yesterday she and Austin had moved all their furniture out of the apartments into the new house.

Tracey had set her old rocker and six-paned mirror in the master bedroom, and that very day Jackson had been able to see his face in the bottom row of mirrors for the first time.

He'd been so pleased with himself and ran to find Emily and tell her how big he was getting.

Now Tracey was getting ready for her simple family wedding. Her wedding outfit was laid out on the four-poster. She smoothed the wide-legged, flowing pants and picked up the lace top in the same eggshell color. She hadn't wanted a fancy dress with all the buttons and layers of tulle, even though that's what Molly tried to talk her into buying. However, when she had tried on the simple outfit, Molly had cried and told her that was exactly what she should wear. Susan, one of the sisters-in-law, poked her head in the door. "Hey. You're going to become my sister-in-law in less than an hour and you're still not ready?"

"I was just about to twist my hair up into a messy bun," Tracey said. "I don't need much time for the rest of getting ready. Are you sure Ellie isn't upset with us for being away on Thanksgiving?"

"Oh, honey," Susan said. "She's so glad to see y'all married and that she gets to keep the kids this week while you're away on a honeymoon that she is dancing on air."

"We didn't remember that we got a whole week off from classes during the holiday when we first talked about a wedding. But"—Tracey lowered her voice—"I'm so glad that we have that much time off."

"What I wouldn't give for a Caribbean cruise." Susan sighed. "You sure you don't want some of us sisters-in-law to go with you?"

"I think we can manage just fine all alone," Tracey said with a smile.

"I just love that outfit." Kelly came into the room and closed the door behind her. "I've been across the hallway fixing Austin's bolo tie. He is a nervous wreck. He's afraid something will happen to prevent this wedding."

"Nothing had better get in the way of it, or I'll break out my redheaded temper. I'm so looking forward to that cruise and spending a whole week with him." Tracey chuckled.

"Where's your garter? Better put it on before we forget," Susan said.

"I'm not wearing one," Tracey said. "I'm wearing my mother's sapphire earrings that she wore on her wedding day for something blue." She pulled back her hair to show the long, dangling blue stones surrounded by diamonds. "For something old, I've got on an old bra, and something new is my lacy underpants."

"Sounds like you've got everything covered, so I'm going back downstairs to help Mom and Molly. They were tearin' around the kitchen in their Sunday-best outfits, daisy corsages, and flour-sack aprons."

Tracey giggled. "That's a funny visual. Did you see the cake? Molly put two dozen real roses on it since that's what my mother had on her wedding cake."

"It's absolutely gorgeous," another sister-in-law said as she entered the room.

"Grandpa's got the tables all set up outside for the supper

afterward. There are sunflowers and daisies in the middle of them all, except the table where you and Austin are sittin'. She insisted on a big bunch of wildflowers and roses there. Grandpa has barbecued everything that lays still. If anyone goes hungry, that's their problem," Susan rattled on. "I said I was going down to help them, but I just remembered. You'll need your bouquet."

"Carolina said she'd bring it up."

As if on cue, Carolina, another sister-in-law, brought in a bouquet of wildflowers tied with a green ribbon. She gently laid it on the dresser. "Looks like you've got about half an hour. Want to get dressed and let me tie that sash on your pants for you? Believe me, all of us sisters-in-law are good at getting a bow tied just right with as many daughters as we've had in the family."

"Yes, please." Tracey pinned her hair up and set a circlet of wildflowers around the messy bun. Then she dropped her robe and got dressed. Carolina tied her sash and then pointed at Tracey's feet. "We've heard of barefoot and pregnant down here in Tom Bean," she said. "But you've got to wear your shoes with an outfit that beautiful."

"Thank you both," Tracey said. "This is the best day in the—"

"Whole world," all the women chimed in together.

Tracey slipped her feet into a pair of ballet flats and looked at her reflection in the long mirror. "I do look like my mother. I wish she were here."

"She is," Carolina said. "She's looking down and loving every minute of this. I'm going back downstairs. See you in a few minutes, and welcome to the family."

"Thank you," Tracey said without taking her eyes off her reflection.

"See you later." The other two women eased out the door, and then Tracey's father knocked on the door and entered the room without waiting.

"You're beautiful," he told her as he took her arm to escort her down the stairs. "You look so much like your mother today that it brings tears to this old man's eyes. And that little Emily looks enough like you to be your natural daughter, instead of your adopted one. Who would've ever thought six years ago when Jackson was just a couple of days old and you brought him to my home the first time that all this would come to pass?"

"Hush, Daddy," she whispered. "You'll make me cry."

"There's our cue. Your mother didn't look at anyone but me, and she smiled when she came down that church aisle to my side. She would be so proud of you today." He stepped through the back door and into the house, which smelled like fresh bread, barbecue, and a flower shop all blended together.

From the time she could see Austin, no one else existed. When they stepped off the bottom step into the great room, Frank took Tracey's arm away from his and gave it to Austin. "Take care of her, son."

"I promise I will," Austin said and led her to the end of the room.

"Dearly beloved." The preacher started the ceremony. "We are gathered here today with Tracey Walker and Austin Miller to celebrate their union."

Tracey was supposed to be listening to the preacher and looking at him, but she couldn't keep her eyes from Austin's.

"Do you, Tracey Dianne Walker, take this man to be your husband?"

"I never thought that this day would come to pass, but I'm glad that Fate or God or the universe brought us back together. I loved you when we were younger. I love you today. I will love you tomorrow. But that's really not long enough. I will love you through all eternity, and if you climb those stairs to the Pearly Gates before I do, then go slow and wait on me at the top, because I don't want to live without you.

So this day I take you to be my husband, to hold you in times of sorrow, to laugh with you in joy, to share my life with you forever. I promise to make a home for you and our children, both present and those to come, and I vow to love you forever," she said.

"Do you, Austin Nelson Miller, take this woman to be your wife?"

"My world is complete this day, Trace. Like you, I'm glad that we get this second chance at happiness, and I will never take it for granted. I've always loved you, from the first time I saw you in the cafeteria at the university. I promise to love you, not just on this special day. I'm not sure eternity is even long enough for all the love I plan to give to you and our children. So this day, I take you, Trace, to be my wife, to hold you in times of sorrow, to laugh with you in joy, to share my life with you forever. I promise to provide a home for you and our children, both present and those to come, and I vow to love you forever and ever with a love that is Red River deep."

"Rings?" the preacher asked.

Austin reached into the pocket of his Sunday-best jeans, brought out matching gold wedding rings, and handed them to the preacher.

"These rings"—the preacher held them up—"are a

symbol of everlasting love, never-ending in a perfect circle. You may each put them on the other's finger, signifying that you are sealing a never-ending marriage in which you will always remember the vows you have said before God and man today."

Tracey slipped Austin's ring on his finger, and then he did the same with hers.

"By the authority vested in me by the great state of Texas, I pronounce you husband and wife," the preacher said. "Austin, you may kiss your bride."

He bent her backwards in a true Hollywood kiss, and then straightened her up to a standing position. "I love you, Mrs. Miller," he said.

"I love you, Austin," she told him.

Read on for a look
at *The Christmas Wish*

Prologue

FROM THE DAY WADE MONTGOMERY BOUGHT THE HOUSE Bridgette Knox grew up in, he had dreams of one day bringing her back to it as his wife. But over time, it was beginning to dawn on him that her dreams and his did not coincide.

Wade had never considered himself a player, but he'd never thought of himself as a loser, either. And yet, in the past six months, Bridgette had laid waste to his ego, his hopes of ever having a relationship with her, and his decision to come back to Blessings. If he had not promised his uncle Dub he'd manage Truesdale's Feed and Seed store, he might have already thrown up his hands and called it quits.

———

On this morning, he'd just finished shaving and paused to look at himself in the mirror. His aunt Nola called him a dark-haired version of Thor. He knew she was referring to some Australian actor named Hemsworth, but Wade didn't see it. He just saw himself. A guy with blue eyes and a dimple in one cheek. Still, he wondered what it was about him that turned Bridgette Knox into an ice princess. He'd gotten the cold shoulder from her so many times, he was beginning to get a complex. He just considered himself a normal single guy in a small southern town, trying to get the attention of the only girl he cared about, and he wasn't so sure she would throw water on him if he was on fire.

Bridgette—sweet Bridgette—had become his Waterloo. She had an excuse every time he asked her out, so he quit asking.

He was trying to come to terms with the fact that maybe it was because he just wasn't her type. She was the biggest failure of his adult life, and it was killing him.

He left home in a mood, and it stayed with him all the way to the feed store. When he saw her car parked in her usual place, his gut knotted, but there was still a tiny seed of hope that had yet to die.

Maybe today is the day she sees me.

Bridgette Knox, a.k.a. Birdie to the people who knew her longest, had a dilemma.

She had a major crush on her boss, but it was complicated. They'd grown up together, but then he'd moved away when they were still in high school, only to show back up in Blessings six months ago to manage the feed and seed store where she worked.

She'd been the bookkeeper there since graduating from high school. She loved her job, and she would always have a soft spot for Dub Truesdale for hiring a nervous teenager with a head for numbers and a glowing letter of recommendation from her business teacher.

But Dub's retirement took them all by surprise, and the guy who haunted Bridgette's dreams, and made her heart flutter just from a simple look, was now her boss.

It made everything weird.

Sometimes she thought Wade felt the same way about her, because he seemed so friendly, and then she'd talk herself out of it because he was friendly to everyone.

So she admired him from afar and kept her feelings locked up tight. The only man she'd been attracted to in years was now the man she answered to at work, and the dilemma remained.

Bridgette was feeling sorry for herself this morning as she pulled up into her parking spot at work. Her steps were dragging as she went in the side door and into her office. She stowed her things and went up front to say hello to the crew and see what, if anything, was new on the day's docket.

It didn't take long for her to get caught up in the customers coming and going, and fending off the teasing she got from being the only female employee in the place.

She was leaning on the counter, listening to one of the old farmers relating a story about his wife and a mean rooster and, like everyone there, waiting to see how the story ended.

"She didn't put up with all that spurrin' and floggin' long," the old man said. "She went after him like a heat-seeking missile, wrung his dang neck, and *bam!* Chicken and dumplings for Sunday dinner."

Bridgette was still laughing when she saw Wade walk in the store.

Wade came in with car keys in one hand and his coffee in the other. The first person he saw was Bridgette. She was standing behind the counter among half a dozen men, her black wavy hair framing that pretty heart-shaped face, and something inside of him snapped.

"Bridgette, when you are finished with what you're doing, please come to my office," he announced, and moved past her with long, steady strides.

She blinked, said her goodbyes to the customer, and headed down the hall, wondering what was wrong.

The door was open.

She walked in.

"Close the door, please," he said.

Bridgette's heart skipped a beat as she pushed it shut.

"What's wrong?" she asked.

"I don't know!" Wade said. "You tell me!"

She was stunned. Wade was never mad at her.

"I don't understand what you're getting at," she said.

Wade dropped down in the chair behind his desk and then looked up at her.

"Neither do I. You're friendly and funny and engaging with every person in Blessings except me. Are you mad because I bought the house where you grew up, or do you just dislike me? I really need to know."

Bridgette was in shock. "Of course I don't dislike anything

about you. I am not mad, and no, I do not hate you. That's
ridiculous."

Wade shoved his hands through his hair in frustration.

"Then do you just want me to quit asking you out? To just
leave you alone? I need to know so I can turn loose of this
dream I had, or find out what the hell is wrong and fix it."

Birdie was shaking inside. She had to ask but was afraid
to hope.

"What dream?"

Wade stood. This was where it could get messy. "The one
where you and I go on dates, and fall in love, and live happy
ever after."

Birdie gasped. "I had no idea... You never said..."

Wade threw up his hands in disbelief. "Bullshit, Bridgette.
How many times have you rejected my invitations?"

There was a lump in her throat and a knot in her stomach
that kept twisting tighter and tighter.

"I thought that was you just being friendly. I didn't want
to get hurt...and you're my boss. I never... It didn't seem right
to..."

His voice softened, and then he sighed. "Well, I was being
friendly because that's how relationships start. And Dub is
still everyone's boss here. I'm just the nephew who agreed to

be manager. Did working for me put me out of the running? Because if that's all that's holding you back, I'll quit my job."

Her eyes welled.

"I don't know what I'm supposed to say. No, I don't want you to quit. Am I fired?"

"Oh, for the love of God! No, you're not fired. What kind of a monster do you think I am? If you don't want anything to do with me personally, then I get it. But six months of giving you time to grieve the loss of your mother and the loss of your family home is all I've got. Your job is fine. I'm fine. You're fine. I guess all I need to know is...am I wasting my time dreaming about you and me ever having a future together?"

Bridgette's hands were wadded into fists and clutched against her stomach. She knew her voice was going to shake. This was like something out of a fairy tale where the prince with the glass slipper finally found the princess it fit.

"No, you're not wasting your time."

Wade sighed, then ended the distance between them when he hugged her.

"Dammit, Bridgette. I did not mean to make you cry. I adore you. I always have...pretty much since first grade. What do I need to do to make it right with you?"

She looked up. "Kiss me?"

So he did.

———————

Two weeks later, they were sitting in Granny's Country Kitchen, waiting for the waitress to bring them their ticket for the meal they'd just eaten. What had taken six months to begin between them had gone into full bloom in two weeks, and it showed.

People in Blessings were starting to talk about Wade and Birdie, Birdie and Wade—but Peanut and Ruby Butterman were the first to ask when they stopped at their table to say hello.

"Hey! I'm sure seeing a lot of you two together these days. Is there something going on here that I don't know about?" Ruby asked.

Wade grinned. "Now, Ruby...you always know what's going on in Blessings before it happens."

Ruby shrugged. "It's not my fault. Sitting in a chair at a hair salon is almost the same as being in a confessional, but you haven't confessed a thing, and I'm asking... *Are* you two—"

"Girl, let them be," Peanut said, and tried to steer Ruby toward the exit.

"Oh, it's okay," Bridgette said. "We *are* doing our best to become 'something,' but not before Wade dared me to stop pretending I didn't know he existed."

"I was getting desperate," Wade said.

Peanut glanced at his wife, remembering their own journey and the struggle it took to get where they were today.

"I know the feeling. I've been there. And now that Ruby has satisfied her curiosity, we're getting out of your hair," Peanut said.

Ruby winked, and then they were gone.

Wade eyed the rosy flush on Bridgette's cheeks.

"So we're working on something, are we?"

"That's how I see it," Bridgette said.

"Then what else can I do to make that something become our thing?" he asked.

"Make love to me."

Wade felt like he'd been punched in the gut. He pulled a handful of bills out of his pocket, tossed them down onto the table, and got up.

Bridgette grasped his hand, holding on tight as he pulled her through the dining room and out into the night.

"My place or yours?" he asked, as Bridgette reached for her seat belt.

"Mine is closer," she said.

Wade drove out of the parking lot and headed across town. He'd been dreaming of this for so long he had the scenario down pat, and then Bridgette up and knocked him off his feet.

When he pulled up into the parking lot at the Cherrystone Apartments, he was seriously glad hers was on the first floor because his legs were shaking too much to climb stairs.

She got out of the car holding the key and, with his hand on her back, unlocked the door into the foyer.

A long hallway ran the lower length of the building, and a set of stairs beside it led to the second floor. Her apartment was the last one on the left at the end of the hall.

Wade glanced down at her as they walked, marveling at the calm on her face. He felt like a lit fuse.

Once inside her place, they abandoned their coats on the sofa and moved toward her bedroom. It was the calmest approach to coming undone that Wade had ever experienced, and it felt right.

But once inside, the bed might as well have had flashing red lights because it was the only thing he saw—until Bridgette began taking off her clothes, and then all he could see was the beautiful woman who'd stolen his heart.

He stripped as she turned back the bed, and then they were lying on their sides, face-to-face. He slid his hand over her belly, up across the mounds of her breast, to the curve of her cheek, then leaned over and kissed her.

"I don't have words for how much I love you," he said.

Bridgette sighed. "Then show me. I ache from the want of you. Make love to me, Wade."

And so he did, tracing the shape of her with his hands, and then his lips, finding the places on her body that made her breath catch and feeling the rapid rising of her pulse beneath his fingertips. And then, with all the grace and restraint he could muster, sliding inside her as she wrapped her legs around his waist, keeping time with the rise and fall of her body as she met him thrust for thrust, until all of their restraint was gone.

Wade went deeper, faster, winding her up so tight she finally broke, leaving him one step behind as he finally shattered within her embrace.

The next level of "them" had just happened, and it was perfect.

Chapter 1

SIXTEEN-YEAR-OLD DUFF MARTIN WAS MISSING, AND HIS older brother, Allen, and his mother, Candi, were in a panic. His bed hadn't been slept in, Allen's car was gone, and it appeared some of Duff's clothes might be missing.

Candi was hysterical.

"Oh my God! What happened? Is this because of last night? We have to call the police!"

"And tell them what, Mom? He took my car and ran away? So do you want him reported as a car thief? Dad's already in prison. We don't need to send Duff down that road, too," Allen said.

Candi sat down on Duff's bed, her shoulders slumped, tears running down her face.

"It's all my fault. Last night, when we began talking about your daddy going to prison, Duff freaked out. I still don't know what I said that set him off."

"He was just six when Dad was sentenced. How much of all that did you ever tell him?" Allen asked.

Candi shrugged and wiped her face. "At the time? Not much. He was too little to understand. And then over the years, he never asked for details. He just knew it was for theft."

Allen sat down beside her and gave her a quick hug. "What exactly were you saying right before he blew up? Do you remember?"

Candi sighed. "Lord...I don't know. I mentioned seeing Selma Garrett's obituary, and he asked who she was, and I think I said...she was the woman who accused Zack of stealing her jewelry. And then Duff got this funny look on his face and asked, 'What jewelry?'"

"Oh yeah," Allen said. "And I added they were family heirlooms, valued at over a quarter of a million dollars, that went missing while Dad was painting at her house."

Candi nodded. "Something about that set Duff off. When he jumped up from the table all pale and shaking, then started hitting himself on the head and crying, I knew something was wrong. I should have talked to him last night, but he wouldn't let me in. And now this!"

"But why would that have upset him? After all this time? And what about all that would have made him run away?" Allen asked.

"I don't know, but he's gone, and I'm scared of what might happen to him," Candi said.

"Does he have access to money?"

Candi gasped. "His college fund!"

"Quick, Mom...check his bank account," Allen said.

Candi pulled up their joint account, checked it, and groaned. "There's a thousand dollars missing."

Allen nodded. "Okay, then he's not about to go robbing some Quick Stop for money. Call him to see if he answers."

"Yes, yes," Candi said, and quickly sent Duff a text.

Allen gave her a quick hug. "Okay. We've reached out. Now we need to wait and see if he responds. The bottom line here is that he's sixteen, so he's a minor. He wasn't abducted, so the cops will call him a runaway. And the only way the police will get involved is if we press charges for him taking the car, and I'm not going to do that. Something is going on with Duff. He's a good kid, and I'm not going to fly off the handle here and make a bad thing worse."

"You're right," Candi said, and then broke into tears again. "But he's just a kid, and we just put up the Christmas tree, and now he's gone."

"So pray, Mama. Pray for a miracle that we get him home."

━━━━━━━━

Duff Martin didn't run away from home, but he was on a mission. Something his mother said last night had triggered a long-forgotten memory. All he could think afterward was *What if it was my fault?* And the only way he could know for sure was to go back to the place where it all began.

So he packed up a bag and headed north, driving out of Florida into Georgia, going back to Blessings, the little Georgia town where he'd spent the first six years of his life. He didn't tell anyone where he was going because, in his sixteen-year-old mind, this was his problem to solve.

He'd snuck out of the house just after 2:00 a.m., arrived in Blessings about 5:00 a.m., and immediately got a room at the only motel. It wasn't the cleanest, but he didn't have money to waste on the nicer bed-and-breakfast he'd seen online, and this place was a roof over his head.

He stretched out on the bed, so tired he ached, but this

wasn't the time to sleep. Now that he was here, he was uncertain where to start. He had memories, but they were vague, and he wasn't sure how much of them was real.

He couldn't remember the house they'd lived in.

He couldn't remember the name of the lady his dad had been working for. He'd heard his mother say it, but he was so freaked out about the rest of the story that it didn't soak in. The only things he could remember for sure were being in first grade at the elementary school and the lady who babysat him after school. Miss Margie. He'd called her Miss Margie.

His first instinct was to start driving the streets of Blessings and see what rang a bell. He wasn't on a schedule, but as soon as the town began opening up, he took off down Main, oblivious to the holiday atmosphere and decorations, and started his first loop through the residential areas, looking for houses and faces he might remember.

When his phone signaled a text and he saw who it was from, he sighed.

They knew he was gone.

———

Even without snow, Christmas spirit was alive and well in Blessings. The little town was in full-on holiday mode.

Decorations were hanging from every streetlight on Main.

There was an ongoing storefront-decorating contest and a trophy to be won for the business that had the best Christmas theme, and the upcoming Christmas parade on Saturday with more trophies to win.

Because snow in this part of Georgia was almost always a no-show, Crown Grocers had brought in its own brand of snow by setting up a snow-cone stand at the north corner of the parking lot, next to the roped-off area where they were selling Christmas trees.

Bridgette could feel the magic of the season all the way to her bones as she drove down Main on the way to work.

In the months since she and Wade had become a couple, the only awkward moment between them had been walking back into the home she'd grown up in and accepting it belonged to him now.

Then as it turned out, it wasn't as hard as she had feared. Her brother Hunt had updated and remodeled it to such a degree before the sale that she soon forgot the old house and saw only the one it was today—the one that belonged to Wade. And the first time they made love in that house, in his bed, memories of the old house were no longer visible to her there.

Making love to Wade was passion at its best, but it was feeling cherished that had put the sparkle in her eyes and the bounce in her step. When she thought about how close she'd come to messing it up, she shuddered. He was now, and would forever be, the best thing to ever happen in her life.

She braked at the stoplight, and while she was waiting for it to turn green, it gave her a few moments to check out the decorations going up in the storefronts. They weren't quite on the level of Bloomingdale's or Saks Fifth Avenue in New York City, but they were Blessings's best, and she couldn't wait to see the finished displays.

The day started out cool—right at fifty degrees, but with a promise to warm up to the mideighties around noon—and she had a busy day ahead of her with end-of-month reports.

December marked the beginning of a busy season at the feed store, including the new gift section Wade had created a few months ago. Among the items available for sale there were little packs of dog and cat toys, halters and spurs for the locals who fancied themselves cowboys, and colorful bandannas, along with a whole series of country-style Christmas ornaments, and Made in Georgia specialties like peach jams and jellies.

Bridgette had always enjoyed working here, but the fire

that gutted the warehouse last year, resulting in the death of a longtime employee, had taken the heart out of all of them. Then Wade came on as manager and changed the vibe to such a degree that the store barely resembled what it had been.

The stoplight turned green, and she drove through the intersection. Once she reached the feed store, she parked and hurried inside out of the cold.

———

Wade was on his way to the Crown to pick up an order of Christmas cookies for the break room, but he was thinking about Bridgette.

They'd spent the weekend together at his house. The house where she'd grown up was now the place where they played house. Cooking together. Watching movies together. Making love in his bed, and on the living room sofa, and in the shower, and wherever else they were when the notion struck. But she'd gone home after Sunday dinner to do the chores needed at her own place, and waking up alone this morning made her absence even more pronounced.

He was looking forward to work, knowing he'd be spending the day with her, as he pulled into the Crown parking lot. Then he saw Bridgette's brother Junior on the far side of the parking lot and waved as he got out. Junior saw him and smiled, then returned to unloading and setting up the new shipment of Christmas trees.

Once inside the store, Wade headed straight to the bakery.

"Hey, Sue. I have an order of Christmas cookies to pick up."

"Morning, Wade. I just boxed them up," she said and went to get them. He took them up front to pay before heading on to the store.

Bridgette's car was already in her usual parking spot when he arrived. He parked and hurried into the store with the cookies, greeting customers and workers alike as he went down the hall to the office area, then paused outside her office, peering at her through the wreath dangling over the window of her door. She was laser-focused on the computer screen, her fingers flying across the keyboard.

He knocked and walked in.

"Hey, sweetheart! I missed you this morning," he said, and then stole a quick kiss.

Bridgette cupped the side of his face.

"I missed you, too."

"I brought cookies for the break room, but you get first dibs. Take out all you want now, because they won't last long."

"Ooh, yum," she said as he opened the box. "I love iced sugar cookies."

"There are some gingerbread men on the bottom. Dig through and get what you want," he added.

"I'll get some out for you, too," Bridgette said, then grabbed a handful of napkins, laid out a sugar cookie and a gingerbread man for herself, and then two each for him. "There, you can take the rest to the break room. I'll put yours in your office."

A couple of hours later, her sugar cookie was gone and the gingerbread man stashed in her desk. She was almost through with the monthly reports when she realized the total between receipts and deposits was off. There was data in the computer showing sales, but the total of monthly deposits didn't balance out, so she went back over her input again, then pulled up the readouts from the front register until she found the exact amount she was off. The transaction was there, but that day's money deposit was short $532.50—the exact amount of a receipt she had for a feed purchase.

Her heart sank.

Either someone pocketed the money or gave away the feed and hoped no one would catch it. In all the years she'd worked here, this had only happened a couple of times, and both times it had been theft.

Once a clerk had pocketed the money, and the other time, a man working in the warehouse had done his buddy a favor, loaded up feed, wrote out a ticket for it to balance out the inventory count, and hoped no one would catch the money missing.

She read the transaction again and saw the register code. It belonged to Donny Corrigan. But that didn't always mean he was the one who'd rung it up. If he'd stepped away from the register to help someone else, any employee could have used it to check a customer out, without keying in their own code. It would be an easy way to take money with no expectation of getting caught.

The next thing Bridgette did was check the time cards to see where Donny was that day, and if he was in the store at that time. She found where he'd clocked in, and then three hours later had clocked out and hadn't come back that whole day.

She frowned, trying to remember why, and then she realized that was the day Donny's wife went into labor with their first baby. He had clocked out, but in his panic, it appeared he had not counted out his till, which left his code in the register, which now made everyone else in the store a possible suspect.

She picked up her phone and called Wade.

Chapter 2

WADE WAS ON THE LOADING DOCK, TALKING TO A CUSTOMER who was waiting for his order, when the call came. When he saw it was Bridgette, he frowned. She never called him like this. She usually came looking for him.

"Excuse me. I need to take this. Good to see you again," he said, and was already talking as he walked away. "Hey, honey, what's up?"

"Can you come to my office?"

"On the way," he said, and hastened his step. The moment he walked in and saw the look on her face, he knew it wasn't going to be good. "What's wrong?"

So she began laying out what she'd found and how she'd found it, explaining Donny's absence during the time of the theft and that it appeared someone had stolen over five hundred dollars from the till while Donny's employee code was active.

"Well, shit, Bridgette. Does this kind of thing happen often?"

She sighed. "Two times in all the years I've been here, but I had a thought. You put up security cameras when the gift shop area went up. Are any of them pointing toward the front register? And if so, how long do we keep footage?"

Wade jumped up and ran back into the store and eyed the cameras again to remind himself. The one over the front door was aimed straight at checkout. He ran back to her office.

"Good call. Bring your notes and come with me."

Bridgette jumped up from her desk, grabbed her pad and pen, and followed him. He was in his office, standing at the little alcove where the security system was set up.

"So, what was the day of the theft?" he asked.

"It was last Thursday," she said.

Wade checked the calendar, then pulled up the stored files and searched for the date.

"And what time was it when Donny clocked out?" Wade asked.

"11:35 a.m.," Bridgette said.

Wade began fast-forwarding. "Okay, got it! Here he is

taking the call. You can see the excitement on his face. Then there you are walking into the store area."

"Yes, he's telling me he needs to go. I wave him on, and that's Josh who comes to stand in for him. Donny clocked out, but he didn't check himself out at the register," Bridgette said. "Now we need to go to 2:17 p.m. That's the time stamp on the receipt that correlates with the exact amount of money missing."

Wade nodded and fast-forwarded again until 2:14. Then they began to watch.

"That's Duke Talbot," Bridgette said, pointing to the customer who came in through the hall from the warehouse. "He's the listed buyer."

Wade points at the footage. "He walks up to the register and hands Josh a credit card. Josh scans it. Duke signs the receipt, gets his copy, and then he's gone. So he didn't pay in cash."

"Wait!" Bridgette said. "Look. Josh just lifted up the cash drawer."

"Son of a bitch," Wade muttered. "He's taking out the bigger bills beneath it. Likely for the same amount. Can you tell if that was a bank debit card or a card from a credit company?"

Bridgette ran back to her computer, did some quick checking, and then came back.

"It was a debit card. That amount showed up the next day in our bank account, so it would not have gone through the store's daily take that day, but it showed up in our account the next day. And it would have all balanced out at the end of the month, if Josh hadn't taken cash from our daily receipts."

Wade was pissed. "My first instinct is to call Josh in and fire his ass. But I'm going to call Uncle Dub first, because he's still the big boss around here. We'll keep this between us for now and wait for Dub to show."

Bridgette started to walk away when Wade stopped her.

"Good job, sweetheart. Good job!"

Bridgette sighed. "I feel bad Josh did this, and right here at Christmas. What's this going to do to his family?"

"He should have thought of that before he stole something that didn't belong to him," Wade said. "Don't feel guilty for someone else's sin."

Bridgette sighed. "You're right. I was just doing my job and caught him failing at his."

"Yes, ma'am, you sure did. It's almost time for lunch. You take an early one. By the time you get back, this will all be over with."

"Josh is still going to know it was me that found it because I'm the one who balances the books," Bridgette said.

Wade frowned. "If he didn't want to get caught, he should have paid it back or packed up and run. Go to lunch."

"I'm going to Granny's. Want me to bring something back for you?" she asked.

"That would be awesome. If it's on the menu today, a chopped brisket sandwich and fries. If not, a burger and fries."

Then he pulled a couple of twenties out of his wallet.

"Lunch is on me today. Leave now and you'll have an hour and a half for lunch, and you have more than earned it."

Bridgette put the money in her pocket. "Thanks for lunch, but I'm sorry you're going to have to do this."

He grimaced. "That's why I get paid the big bucks."

Bridgette went back to her office long enough to save the reports and printout copies, then logged out of her computer, grabbed her coat and purse, and left through the side door.

Wade was in the office, already calling Dub. The phone rang a couple of times, and then his uncle answered.

"Hello?"

"Uncle Dub, it's me. We have a problem at the store, and I wanted to talk to you before I acted on it."

"What's wrong?" Dub asked.

"Josh King stole over five hundred dollars out of the till. Bridgette caught the discrepancy when she was doing the end-of-month reports, and we checked security footage and caught him in the act."

"Josh? Son of a gun! I would not have believed he would do something like that."

"If it wasn't for Bridgette checking details, it would have fallen on Donny Corrigan's shoulders. He was logged into the register when he got the call that his wife had gone into labor last week. He clocked himself out, but he forgot to log out on the register, and Josh stepped up and began checking people out without changing the code. I guess he thought we wouldn't know who'd done it, since it was Donny's code but he was gone. Josh obviously forgot about the security cameras. They haven't been up that long. Look, I have no problem firing him, but I want to know if you want me to press charges or—"

"I'm coming down to the store. We'll be doing this together. And I'll decide on the way about having him arrested. Are you okay with me stepping in on this when you're in charge?" Dub asked.

Wade didn't hesitate. "You're still the boss, Uncle Dub.

You're the owner. I am your manager, and your decisions will always be the ones I go by."

"Good enough. I'll be there in about ten minutes. What I want you to do is call Josh to your office and then wait there with him. I don't want him taking off for lunch. Don't let on you know. Just tell him I need to talk to him," Dub said.

"Yes, sir," Wade said. "I'll page him right now. See you in a few."

———

Josh King was in the warehouse loading chicken feed for a customer and wishing he'd worn a lighter-weight shirt. He was already getting too warm and was planning to change shirts when he went home for lunch.

"Okay, buddy," Josh said as he loaded the last sack into the back of the pickup. "There's your twenty bags. Sign here."

The man signed his name, took the customer copy, and got in his truck and drove away.

Josh stepped inside the warehouse office, laid the store copy in a tray on the desk, and was going to wash his hands when the pager squawked, and then he heard Wade's voice.

"Josh King to the main office, please."

Josh's heart skipped a beat, and then he told himself it

didn't have to mean anything and walked through the main store and down the hall to the office area with his chin up and a strut in his step. The door was open. He paused on the threshold.

"Hey, Wade, what's up?" he asked.

Wade glanced up. "Come in and shut the door."

A chill washed through Josh, but he didn't let on. Instead, he shut the door and walked to the desk.

Wade pointed at a chair on the other side of his desk.

"Sit."

Josh sat, but he was still playing dumb.

"What's going on, Boss?"

"Dub wants to talk to you. He's on the way."

Josh looked straight at Wade. "About what?"

Wade said nothing and stared him down.

At that point, Josh began to panic. *Shit. Shit. Shit. Say nothing. Play it cool. Donny's employee code is all over the sales. They can't prove a damn thing.*

The next five minutes were the longest five minutes of Josh's life. By the time Dub walked into the office, he was sweating.

"Dammit, Dub. What the hell are y'all playing at?" Josh asked.

Wade stood. "Your seat, sir," he said, and moved aside as Dub eased himself down behind the desk.

"Why?" Dub asked.

Josh frowned. "Why what?"

"Why did you steal from me?" Dub asked.

"I didn't steal shit from you!" Josh shouted, and jumped up, which was a mistake because seconds later Wade's hands were on his shoulders.

"Sit your ass back down in the chair. Being mad you got caught isn't going to change what you did."

Josh felt the grip all the way to his bones and dropped back into the chair with a thud.

"I didn't take your money," Josh muttered.

"Except you did," Dub said. "You're not a smart thief. I don't know why you thought you'd get away with it. We already know Donny Corrigan's employee code is on the sale receipt, but the problem is Donny clocked out hours earlier because his wife went into labor. He just forgot to log out of the register, and you took advantage of his error to steal from me and lay the blame on him."

"I–I... If you have money missing, it could have been anyone. Why are you picking on me?" Josh cried.

Wade was leaning against the wall with his hands in

his pockets, watching a man's life coming apart before his eyes.

"I guess you forgot about the security cameras," Wade said. "There's one over the front door aimed straight at the register. We caught the whole thing, from the time Duke Talbot walked out to you lifting the cash drawer and pulling big bills out from beneath."

All the color faded from Josh's face.

"I...uh...well, hell," he said, and then ducked his head.

Dub was disgusted. "I'm gonna ask you one more time. Why? After all these years, why did you think it was suddenly okay to steal from me? I never treated you any way but right."

Josh scrubbed his hands over his face and then swallowed past the knot in his throat and shrugged.

"I owed a debt I couldn't pay. I didn't want to get beat up."

Dub looked up at Wade. "Call the PD for me, Wade."

"Yes, sir," Wade said. He pulled up the number from his contacts and made the call.

Avery Ames, the day dispatcher, answered.

"Blessings PD."

"Avery, this is Wade Montgomery. We caught a thief here

at the store, and we're pressing charges. Can you please send an officer to pick him up? We're in the office."

"Yes, sir, dispatching now," he said.

Wade heard the call go out, and then Avery was back on the line.

"They're on the way. Do you need an ambulance?" he asked.

"No. We're all fine...except for the dumbass in here with us," Wade said.

"Yes, sir," Avery said, and disconnected.

Josh moaned. "I'll pay it back. Don't press charges. I can't go to jail. It's coming up Christmas. What's my wife gonna think? And my kids. Please."

"You should have thought of all that before you stole money from the place where you work," Wade said.

"Out of curiosity, how did you get in that kind of debt?" Dub asked.

Wade frowned. "Did it have anything to do with poker?"

Josh slumped without answering.

Dub looked at Wade in shock. "How did you know that?"

"Josh brags when he wins and comes to work hungover when he loses. I never said anything because he's never come to work drunk, and what a man does on his own time is his business, but after knowing he stole the money, I guessed the rest," Wade said.

"So your wife and kids are really far down on your list of important things to care for," Dub said.

"I'm sorry," Josh said.

"Tell that to your family," Dub said.

Wade glanced out the window and saw a patrol car pulling up to the store.

"They're here," he said.

A few moments later they heard footsteps coming up the hall, and then two officers walked in.

Dub pointed at Josh. "This man stole over five hundred dollars from me, which makes it a felony in the State of Georgia. I'm pressing charges, and I'll follow you to the station to fill out the paperwork."

One officer pulled Josh out of the chair and began cuffing him as the other one read him his rights.

Josh's head was down, his steps dragging as they marched him up the hall, then out through the store and into their car.

"Thanks," Dub said, and gave Wade a quick thump on the shoulder. "You did good, Wade, and you tell Birdie this makes three thieves she's found out since she came to work for me. She hasn't had a raise in years, and I think she's due. Tell her to add four hundred dollars a month to her salary."

"Yes, sir," Wade said. "I'm sure she'll be very appreciative."

"As am I," Dub said. "I'm going by the station now, before I go home."

Wade watched Dub as he left by the side door, his steps dragging as he walked, and then he got in his car and drove away.

———

Duff had driven up and down streets to the point he felt like he was making people nervous. Blessings was small. A stranger was easy to spot. Only he wasn't really a stranger. Just someone who'd been gone a very long time.

By the time noon came around he was hungry, so he headed straight for Granny's Country Kitchen because it was the only real café in town and because he remembered it from before. Once he was seated and had ordered his food, he began watching faces, looking for anyone who looked familiar, but it soon became obvious that he'd been too young and too many years had passed. Without knowing their names, he couldn't identify anyone. So he sat and watched, and when his food finally came, he transferred his attention to that.

He was almost through eating when a young, dark-haired woman walked in. Something about her seemed familiar, and after she was seated and studying the menu, he blatantly stared.

She was someone from before. Someone he'd known.

━━━━━━━

Bridgette was still struggling with the revelations of the theft when she got to Granny's, but the delightful aromas that met her at the door shifted her focus.

Sully Raines was manning the register for his mother, Lovey, who owned Granny's. He looked up at Bridgette as she entered.

"Hello, Birdie. Are you dining alone or meeting someone?"

"I'm alone," she said. "A small table anywhere is fine."

"Gotcha," Sully said. "Follow me," he added, and led her through the dining room to a table for two near the front windows. "Your waitress will be here shortly. The special is baked ham and two sides." He left a menu and hurried back to the lobby.

Bridgette was still trying to decide what she wanted when Lovey showed up with a glass of water, a basket of Mercy's famous biscuits, and an apology.

"Hi, Birdie. Sorry for the delay. I'm short a waitress today, and I'm way out of practice. What do you want to drink?"

"Oh, sweet tea, for sure. And I think I'll have the baked ham, with fried okra and mashed potatoes and gravy. I'll also need a brisket sandwich and an order of fries to go."

"Got it," Lovey said. "I'll turn in the to-go order in a bit. Enjoy the biscuits."

Bridgette didn't have to be prompted twice. Mercy Pittman was the baker at Granny's. Her baking skills were famous now, but it was her biscuits that had put her on the map.

Bridgette broke one of the biscuits in half, buttered both pieces, and then took her first bite. Light as a feather, dripping in melted butter—delicious.

Lovey came back with her drink, and while Bridgette was waiting for her food, she noticed a young teenage boy—a stranger to Blessings—staring at her from across the room.

She thought nothing of it and looked away.

When her food came, she ate without looking up, and when Lovey brought the ticket and her to-go order, she left a tip and got up to leave. Even without glancing his way, she knew he was still watching her, but then forgot about it as she headed back to work, wondering what had happened while she was gone.

She didn't have long to wonder. The moment she walked in, it was obvious the confrontation had occurred. Employees were bunched together talking, and there was an instant hush when the door opened, until they saw it was her.

One employee, a man named Roger Brown, started talking so fast he ran out of breath and had to stop in the middle of a sentence and inhale so he could finish.

"Whoa, Birdie! You missed all the excitement! The cops came and hauled Josh King off in handcuffs and... Wade said Josh stole money and Wade caught it on that camera over the door."

Joe Trainor, who worked in the warehouse, punched Roger on the shoulder.

"Dang it, Roger. Who do you think discovered the money was missing? Birdie does end-of-the-month reports every month. And when things don't balance, she goes looking for why. You can't put nothin' over on this girl. I've been here a long time, and this isn't the first time she's found a...a..."

"Discrepancy?" Bridgette said.

"Yeah! That!" Joe said.

Bridgette nodded. "I did know there was money missing, but Wade is the one who discovered who did it. I'm just sorry it happened."

Roger shook his head. "Josh is the one who's gonna be sorry. Him and his stupid poker games. He's addicted, that's what."

Bridgette didn't want to be in the middle of their gossip and used Wade's lunch as an excuse to move on.

"Gotta take the boss his lunch and get back to work," she said, and went down the hall to Wade's office.

The door was open. He was on the phone. He waved her in, gave her a thumbs-up for the food. She tiptoed in, left the sack and his change on the desk, blew him a kiss, and went back to work.

About a half hour later, Wade came in and kissed the back of her neck as she was sitting at the computer, and then sat down in the chair on the other side of her desk.

"Thank you for bringing my lunch."

She shivered. "You're welcome."

"Uncle Dub says to tell you good job! And he's giving you a raise. The next time you make out your own paycheck, add four hundred dollars a month to it."

Bridgette's eyes widened. "Are you serious?"

Wade smiled. "Yes, ma'am. That's what he said."

"Oh wow! That's a wonderful Christmas present to me. Please tell him thank you."

Wade nodded. "I will. I've got to go make some calls. The company we buy salt blocks from lost our shipment."

———————

Dub had filled out all of the paperwork and signed the complaint against Josh King. He didn't have to, but he felt it was his duty to tell Josh's wife what had happened and left the police station with a heavy heart.

Josh and his family lived a couple of blocks from the elementary school, in a pretty white house with blue shutters. Dub knew the kids would be at school today, and he also knew Josh's wife, LaJune, was a stay-at-home mom. At least he could talk to her without the children present.

He pulled up in the drive, eyed the cheery little Santa Claus hanging on their door, and got out, anxious to get this over with.

He knocked, and a few moments later, the door swung inward.

LaJune King recognized Dub and frowned. In all the years that Josh had worked at the store, his boss had never come calling.

"What's wrong?" she asked.

"May I come in?" Dub asked.

She sighed and stepped aside as Dub entered.

"Take a seat," she said, indicating the sofa just to Dub's right. Then she sat in a nearby chair beside their Christmas tree, her face turning paler by the minute as her hands fisted in her lap. "Just spit it out. You wouldn't be here if Josh hadn't done something wrong."

"I'm sorry to have to tell you this, but Josh stole something over five hundred dollars from me. We caught it on the security camera."

She moaned, but her gaze never wavered. "He gambles," she said.

"Yes, ma'am, so I found out. He admitted it and said it was to pay a gambling debt. He showed no remorse whatsoever. I had him arrested."

LaJune reeled where she sat, clutching the arms of the chair she was in. Her voice was shaking.

"I'd like to say I am surprised, but I'm not. One wrong road always leads to another. I couldn't stop him. Maybe jail will. I am so sorry. I'm afraid I don't have the money to pay you back."

Dub hurt for her situation. "I do not expect you to, LaJune. It is not your debt. And I'm sorry, too. Are you going to be able to manage here on your own?"

"No, but my parents have a little farm on the other side of

Savannah." She sighed and wiped the tears running down her cheeks. "This is pretty much the last straw for me. The kids and I can go there until I figure out what to do."

Dub nodded. "I don't know what your situation is here, and I know paychecks went out yesterday, but considering Josh gambled, you might be short for the month. I want you to have this, too," he said, and pulled a check out of his shirt pocket. "This is from my personal account."

He got up and laid it in her lap, then briefly patted her shoulder. "Do me a favor and don't bail him out of jail with this. I'm sorry as I can be to give you this news. I wish you and your children well."

LaJune was crying openly now. "Thank you for your generosity. You didn't have to do this."

Dub sighed. "Well, if I ever hope to sleep again, then yes, ma'am, I do. I'll see myself out."

He walked out, quietly closing the door behind him, and could hear her sobbing as he walked off the porch.

"Sorry-ass man," Dub muttered, then got in his car and drove home. He had to tell Nola what had happened, and that he'd just given a good sum of money away today. There were no secrets between him and his girl, ever, and forty something years into a marriage, he wasn't going to start.

Chapter 3

Josh King was finally booked into jail and begging Deputy Ralph Herman to let him make a phone call.

"I need to call my wife and tell her to get me a lawyer!" Josh said.

Chief Lon Pittman had been at lunch when he got the call about the arrest and immediately returned to the station. He walked into the jail area just as Josh was making his demands.

The deputy glanced up as Lon walked in.

"Afternoon, Chief. Josh wants to make a phone call."

"I heard," Lon said. "I've got this."

Ralph nodded. "Yes, sir. I'll be going back on patrol," he said, and left the building.

Lon pulled out his cell phone. "What's your number?"

Josh told him, and when the call began to ring, Lon slipped his phone between the bars.

"Don't screw with me, Josh, or you'll regret it," Lon warned.

Josh nodded and put the phone up to his ear, waiting for the call to be answered. It rang, and rang, and rang, and he was about to panic when he finally heard LaJune's voice.

"Hello?"

"Hey, baby, it's me. Listen, I'm in jail, and I need you to get me a lawyer. I'll explain everything later, but—"

"You don't need to explain anything," she snapped. "Mr. Truesdale already paid me a visit. You are a sorry son of a bitch, and I am not going to take the food out of my babies' mouths to pay a lawyer anything. You can get a free lawyer assigned by the court, and I hope you rot in jail for what you've done to us."

Josh blinked. The line went dead. She'd hung up on him!

He handed the phone back to Lon through the bars.

"I'm gonna be needing one of them court-appointed lawyers," he mumbled.

Lon nodded. "I'll let the proper authorities know. They'll assign one to you. Meanwhile, enjoy."

Josh dropped onto the cot, his hands clasped between his

knees. He'd never planned on spending Christmas in jail, and he had a strong feeling that when he got out, there wouldn't be anyone to go home to.

———————

As soon as LaJune hung up the phone, she got her jacket and the extra set of car keys and left the house. It was about a fifteen-minute walk to get to the feed store. The truck in the driveway hadn't worked in months, and Josh damn sure wasn't going to be needing the car. The air was still a little chilly, so she walked faster to warm up.

As she was nearing Main Street, her cell phone rang. She glanced at caller ID and then rolled her eyes. What were the odds? Then she answered.

"Hey, Mom."

"Hi, baby. Daddy and I were talking about the upcoming holidays and wanted to check in with you. I just got word from your brother that he and his family will be here for dinner on Christmas day. Are y'all still planning on coming, too? It would be wonderful if I could have both my babies home for Christmas."

LaJune swallowed past the lump in her throat.

"The kids and I will be there, but Josh just got arrested

and is sitting in jail as we speak. I'm walking to the feed store to get our car."

"Oh my God! What did he do?" her mother asked.

"Stole money from his job and got caught on video doing it, and all because of his damn gambling. He had a debt he couldn't pay, and now here we are. I'm leaving him, Mom. This is the last straw."

"I'm so sorry, LaJune. You and the kids come home. We've got the whole upstairs in this house just begging for little footsteps on the floors again."

"Oh, Mom...thank you. I don't want to be a burden, and it won't be forever. But I need a place to be so I can regroup. I'll need to get a job and save up some money to get a place," LaJune said.

"We'll figure it out together," her mother said. "Do you want us to come get your things?"

"I'm not taking anything but ourselves, the car, and our clothes. Our old truck won't run, so if Josh wants a ride, he'll finally have to fix it."

"If you're going to do this, don't wait until he bonds out of jail. I'm afraid he'll hurt you when he finds out you're leaving."

"He would never hurt me physically, but this broke my

heart. The kids are in school right now. I'll have everything loaded up by the time they get home. Leaving this abruptly will be hard, but going to see Grandma and Grandpa will make them happy. I'll start them in school there when the semester begins after the first of the year, and Josh can figure out the mess he made of our lives on his own."

LaJune heard her mother sigh.

"I love you, baby. It's going to be okay," her mother said.

"I love you, too, Mom, and thank you for always being there for us."

LaJune hung up, then cried all the way to the feed store, got their car, and drove home.

One hurdle crossed.

About a thousand more to go.

———————

It was quitting time, and Bridgette was shutting down her office when Wade appeared in the doorway.

"Hey, darlin'. Wanna go with me to get a Christmas tree for the store? I'll throw in a snow cone for your trouble."

"Oooh, yes!" Bridgette said.

"Do you want to take your car home first, or leave it here and I bring you back to get it later?"

"Are you going to bring the tree back here to the store?"

He nodded.

"Then I'll leave it here."

She grabbed her jacket and purse and followed him through the store as he locked up access doors and made sure the security cameras were working. Wade noticed the pensive look on her face and stopped long enough to give her a quick hug.

"This was a weird day, wasn't it, honey? Are you okay about everything that happened?"

She sighed. "Yes. Just sorry for Josh's family. I know LaJune and the kids well enough to visit with them when I see them around. This makes me sad for them."

Wade pushed a curl from her forehead, then brushed a kiss across her lips.

"I think Uncle Dub was feeling the same. He called me a couple of hours ago to let me know that he went by Josh's house. He thinks they were having a hard time of it because of Josh's gambling."

Bridgette gasped. "Gambling? Is that why he did it?"

Wade nodded. "Dub thinks this will likely end their marriage. He said she has family up around Savannah. However, that means a family is leaving Blessings."

Bridgette sighed. "People come and people go, and life

goes on." Then she gave Wade a quick hug. "I'm just glad you came back to Blessings."

He wrapped his arms around her. "And I'm glad you were still here, even if it did take half a year and me throwing something of a fit to get you to notice me."

Bridgette shook her head. "You are never going to let that go, are you?"

"Maybe one day," Wade said, and then kissed her. "Now, let's get the rest of this place locked up and go get a Christmas tree. I want to display those ornaments we have for sale, and the best way to do that is decorate a tree with them."

"Oh...I want to help," she said.

Wade grinned. "Oh! You are officially in charge of decorating."

They left the feed store arm in arm, got in the store truck they used for in-town deliveries, and then went straight to the Crown.

"What do you want to do first...snow cone or tree?" Wade asked as he parked.

"Let's do both. Get snow cones to eat while we look at trees. Just let me put on my jacket. Eating that shaved ice is going to make me cold, but it will put me in the Christmas mood for sure."

The snow-cone stand looked like a little brown cuckoo-clock with snow on the roof. The steep slope of the pointed roof had ornate gingerbread trim, and the place where the cuckoo would have come out was the window where the orders were taken.

The workers inside the stand were dressed like elves, with green suits and pointed hats, and the menu of available flavors posted on the wooden sign beside it was straight out of the North Pole.

- » Rudolph's Nose—cherry flavor
- » Christmas Tree—lime flavor
- » Candlelight Bright—lemon-pineapple flavor
- » Heavenly Blue—raspberry flavor
- » Starlight White—coconut flavor
- » Santa Wrecked the Sleigh—combo of all flavors

There were small tables with folding chairs set up around the stand where people sat and visited and a short line at the window.

"What's your poison?" Wade asked as they approached the stand.

"Candlelight Bright!" Bridgette said.

Wade grinned. "Go say hi to your brother. I'll get in line to order."

Bridgette took off across the lot toward the Christmas trees and noticed Junior loading up a tree for Jack Talbot. It would be Jack and Hope's first Christmas as parents. Bridgette shivered longingly. Wade and babies sounded wonderful to her.

As she waited for Junior to finish the transaction, she couldn't help but notice the confidence he had about him now—a drastic change from the way he'd been before. It was a tragedy their mama had to die before the secret that had devastated the family was finally revealed and resolved. But after it all came about, it was as if someone had freed Junior from an emotional prison. He had a steady job now, had finished his GED, and had resurrected his personal life as well. He'd been dating a sweet little woman named Barrie Lemons who lived in the Bottoms, and finally moved in with her about five months ago. Barrie had two small children—Lucy, who was school age, and Freddy, who was still a toddler—and Junior was smitten by all three of them.

And then Junior saw Bridgette and came running to give her a quick hug.

"Hi, Birdie!"

"Hi, Junior. How's it going?" she asked.

"Goin' good, honey, goin' good, but we heard there was some kind of commotion at the feed store today. Cops showed up and everything. What happened? Were you in any danger?"

"No. Someone just stole some money and got caught," Bridgette said.

"Ooh, that was stupid," Junior said, and then changed the subject. "I see you're here with your sweetie. I bet I know what kind of snow cone you're getting."

Bridgette grinned. "And that would be what?"

"That lemon one," he said.

Bridgette laughed. "How would you know that?"

"Even as a kid, you were always sucking on a lemon. Made my jaw hurt just looking at you, but you sure did love 'em."

"Guilty," she said. "And here it comes, delivered by my one and only."

Junior smiled. "It's good to see you happy, Sis."

Bridgette patted the side of his cheek. "I'm glad you're happy, too. Are you and Barrie taking the kids to the Christmas parade this Saturday?"

"We have to. That's all Lucy has talked about for a week."

"Then I'll see you there. The guys at the store are making

some kind of a float, and I have been informed I will be riding on it. Lord only knows what it will be."

At that point, Wade walked up beside her.

"Evening, Junior. Here's your snow cone, sugar, and you'll hear all about the float tomorrow. Right now, we're gonna buy a Christmas tree for the store."

"We have sizes from four to eight feet tall. What size would you be wanting?" Junior asked.

Wade pointed at Bridgette, who was nose deep in her snow cone.

"This is the lady in charge of that. As soon as she gets over the brain freeze from that monstrous bite, I'll let her tell you."

Bridgette would have laughed, but she was too busy riding out the pain in her head from the bite she'd just taken.

"Ooh, my bad," she said. "The snow cone is so good, but I did not allow for that. What kind did you get?"

Wade showed her. "I couldn't decide, so I got Santa Wrecked the Sleigh. It has some of all of them. Want a bite?"

Bridgette eyed the conglomeration of colors and wrinkled her nose. "I'll pass."

Both men laughed, then Wade began eating his as they started through the lot, looking at shapes and sizes of the trees, trying to decide between pines or firs, with Bridgette ignoring most of what they were saying. She was envisioning the ornaments they had at the store and wanted the perfect tree to use for display.

They had circled the lot and were working their way inward when she spotted a tall, sturdy one with a solid shape.

"That one," she said, pointing. "It will be perfect in that corner by the gift area."

"Load her up," Wade said, and Bridgette followed along behind them.

She took a last bite of the cone and then dropped what was left in the trash bin near the stand as they walked away. As she turned to catch up, she saw the stranger from Granny's again. This time, he was leaning against a car, his arms folded across his chest, staring at her.

She stopped and stared back until he was the one to break his gaze and walk away.

It bothered her that this was happening, and that he was still in Blessings, even though he had made no advances or threatened her in any way. And once again, she shook off concern and hurried to catch up.

They took the tree back to the store, left it propped up in the corner, then locked the store, and walked to the parking lot.

"That was fun. Thanks for taking me along, but tomorrow I fully expect to find out what the big secret is about me and that float," Bridgette said.

Wade grinned. "You're going to be the hit of the parade."

Bridgette shook her head. "No. Santa is going to be the hit."

"Who does Santa?" Wade asked.

"Peanut is Santa again this year, and Ruby is Mrs. Claus, or so I heard."

"Awesome. Ever since my parents passed, I've been kind of lost as to what to do about holidays. Uncle Dub and Aunt Nola are the only blood relatives I have left, and I'm excited about all of this and making memories with you," Wade said.

Bridgette felt the pang of knowing this would be her family's first Christmas without their mother, Marjorie, too.

"It doesn't matter how old you are when you lose both parents... You feel like an orphan, don't you? But we have each other now and new memories to make."

Wade hugged her. "I love you, Bridgette. So much. And if we weren't standing out in public here, I'd kiss you senseless."

She laughed. "Propriety is boring, but I guess we can't be

scandalous right here before Christmas and get on Santa's bad side. I'll see you tomorrow, and you *will* tell me about the float."

He grinned. "I'll see you tomorrow, for sure."

She shook her head, then got in her car and drove away.

Wade sighed. He had to go by the cleaners and then stop off at the hardware store, then head back to the warehouse behind the store where they were building the float. His day was far from over.

―――――――――――

Duff Martin was rattled. That lady at the Crown had called his bluff and stared him down, but she looked so familiar, and it was driving him crazy. Why couldn't he remember?

He was beginning to realize he couldn't do this on his own. He should have told his mom and Allen what he was doing, but he still wasn't sure that what he remembered had anything to do with why his dad was in prison.

It was getting late and chilly, so he went into the Crown and got some food from the deli, then took it back to his motel. He needed to let his mom know he was okay. He wasn't going to tell her what he was doing, but he didn't want her thinking he was dead. So as soon as he got back to his room, he put his groceries on the table and sat down on the side of the bed and called.

———————

Candi was too upset and too rattled to focus on work and had called in sick, letting Allen take her car to work instead. And now every time her phone rang and it wasn't Duff, the knot in her belly grew tighter.

It was almost sundown when her cell phone rang, and when she saw Duff's number pop up, she couldn't answer fast enough.

"Hello! Duff? Honey?"

"Hi, Mom."

"Oh my God...where are you? Why did you run away? Was it something I said? If it was, I'm so sorry. Just come home. We'll figure it out."

"No, Mom, no. You didn't do anything wrong and I'm not in trouble. But there's something I have to do. I can't say more now, but I'm not doing anything illegal. I promise I'm not in trouble."

Candi was crying now. "Where are you, Duffy?"

"I'll call you again in a day or two," Duff said. "Just don't worry."

In a last-ditch effort to get him back, Candi threw out the obvious.

"You're missing school."

"Tell them it was a family emergency. I'll make up my classes, I promise."

Candi sighed. "I don't like this. I don't like lying to people."

"I'm not lying about anything," Duff said. "Just trust me on this. If I'm right, it may be the best thing that has happened to us in a really long time. Tell Allen I'm sorry I took his car without asking, but I'm taking good care of it. I love you. Bye."

And then he was gone.

Candi looked at the dark screen on her phone and then clutched it to her breast.

At least she'd finally heard from him. At least now she knew he wasn't in trouble. And he'd given her no choice but to trust him.

But Duff was feeling a lot of what his mother was feeling. Sad, worried, unsettled, and guilty. More guilty than he'd ever thought possible.

Tomorrow he would go to the local library. If they had back issues of the local paper, the story of his dad's arrest and incarceration should be in it. He needed to know the whole truth before he took the next step.

━━━━━━━━━━

Wade went home long enough to change into old clothes and then headed to the empty warehouse where they were building the float.

"Did you bring your hammer? We're building a fence here," Roger yelled as Wade walked in.

Wade just grinned. "Just remember to build it in sections, like short sideboards, so we can slide them into place on the flatbed Saturday morning before the parade."

"If the guy doesn't show up with your critter, what are we gonna do?" Roger asked.

"The guy will send a crew with the critter, as you call it, and load it on our trailer. The man who owns the company is a college friend. He guaranteed they would be here by 7:00 a.m. Saturday, and I'll be waiting. They will stay for the parade, then load it up and take it back. I just have to get power to it. I have a generator that will do the job, and we can hide it with some hay bales."

"Birdie is so going to be the hit of this parade," Roger said.

Wade knew Bridgette. She was going to love everything about this. Tomorrow was Friday. The parade was Saturday. There was no time to waste.

———————

Bridgette went to sleep thinking about Wade, but when she dreamed, she dreamed of the stranger who was following her, and when she woke up the next morning, he was still on her mind. He reminded her of someone. If only she knew his name, maybe that would trigger a memory. If she saw him again, she was going to confront him, because this was beginning to get creepy.

She thought about telling Wade and then didn't. If it was totally innocent, she didn't want to get the kid in trouble. Maybe he was just here visiting family for the holidays and bored. Maybe they just happened to be in the same place at the same time twice. So what? Blessings was a small town, and strangers were noticeable. That had to be it.

Now that she'd talked herself out of being concerned, she went to get ready. She was anxious to find out what the float was about and what she was supposed to wear. Probably overalls, or jeans, or maybe a red plaid shirt and a Santa hat. Something farm-related, for sure.

She ate a bowl of cereal, checked the weather, and headed to the car. Office work was on hold. Today she got to decorate the Christmas tree.

She drove slowly up Main, eyeing the window fronts with delight. The contest was getting serious. There were some awesome displays.

When she saw the display at the Curl Up and Dye, she laughed out loud. Ruby had a store mannequin in the window and had dressed it in an old-fashioned, jade-green prom dress—the strapless kind with a long, poofy skirt covered in ruffles. The skirt billowed out from the waist like a dainty little bell, thanks to an old hoop underskirt. Ruby, being Ruby, had spray-painted an old wig forest green and put it on the mannequin, added a gold tiara, then draped it from head to toe with flashing, multicolored Christmas lights, as if the mannequin had become the Christmas tree. And she'd surrounded her with boxes elaborately wrapped to look like gifts, sprayed artificial snow around the outer edges of the window as a frame, and had silver icicles dangling from the eaves outside of the storefront.

Driving further, the window of the flower shop was a mass of poinsettias in every color, displayed on tables and stools of different heights. And there was an oversize Elf on the Shelf sitting beneath the spreading leaves of a white poinsettia, waving.

The hardware store was Bridgette's favorite. They'd created a Santa's workshop with little mechanical elves looking like they were making toys, and so it went all the way down the street. Whoever had thought about the storefront contest had really put the zip in Christmas this year. Blessings didn't need snow to get in the spirit. It was everywhere. Even the police cruisers were sporting Christmas wreaths on the grills.

By the time she got to the feed store, Bridgette had an idea of how she wanted the tree to look. And when she pulled up and parked and saw the big green wreath with a huge red bow hanging on the door, she grinned.

In all the years she'd worked for Dub, he'd never done anything like this. Wade was good for Dub, good for business, and so good for her it made her ache.

She jumped out and went in the side door to stow her things in her office. The first thing she saw when she walked in was the long box on top of her desk. Curious, she opened it and began pulling out the different items—red jeans, a red-and-white-plaid shirt, a black bandanna, and a pair of black boots. She opened a big square box beside it and grinned.

A red cowboy hat. She'd definitely be noticeable, no matter what the float looked like.

Still grinning, she put everything back in the box, set it aside, booted up the computer, and then headed into the store.

Wade already had the tree in a stand, and when he saw her, he waved her over.

"Morning, darlin'. You're just in time. Do you want these clear lights on the tree so that all it does is twinkle, or do you want the colored lights?"

"Oooh, the clear ones. That way nothing will be competing with the ornaments," Bridgette said.

Two of the men came in from the warehouse, both of them grinning.

"Did you tell her yet?" they asked.

Wade shook his head. "No. She just got here."

Bridgette grinned. "Tell me what? I just saw the clothes you want me to wear. Are you talking about the float?"

"Yes, they're talking about the float. So what do you think of the outfit?"

"I think it's cute, and definitely fit for a feed-and-seed-store float. So tell me what it's going to look like."

Wade took a deep breath. "How does riding a mechanical bull down Main Street strike you?"

Bridgett's mouth dropped. "For real?"

"Yes, please," Wade said. "It's a big red bull named Rudolph, and we're going to have it on the slowest, safest speed. Basically, you'll just be hanging on and waving that hat and being cute."

Bridgette blinked. At that point, every man on the premises was standing in the store, waiting for her answer.

"Holy cow," she mumbled.

"Ummm, no, it's a bull," Wade said.

Bridgette burst out laughing. "I'm in."

Wade clapped his hands and then swung her off her feet.

"We're gonna win the trophy for best float, I guarantee... and we're going to put it on the shelf right there behind the register, between the dewormer meds and the ointment for sore teats."

The men whooped and started clapping and laughing.

"Outstanding," Bridgette said. "But it's gonna cost you."

Wade grinned. "Name it and it's yours. Now let's decorate a tree. The rest of you guys, back to work."

They were still laughing and talking as they dispersed to their regular jobs, leaving Donny up front to man the register, while Wade began stringing the lights and Bridgette started gathering up two of every ornament they had for sale to put on the tree.

Chapter 4

DUFF DIDN'T GET MUCH SLEEP.

His mattress was lumpy, and the couple in the room next door fought off and on all night. He missed home. He missed his mom and waking up to the smell of bacon and coffee, and he even missed Allen's gentle nagging.

He showered, got dressed, then ate a honey bun, drank a pint-size carton of milk, and called it breakfast before he left the motel.

When he got in the car, he immediately noticed he was low on fuel, so his first stop was at the gas station to fill up.

"Twenty dollars on pump four, please," he said as he went up to the counter to pay.

The clerk rang up the sale and turned on the pump as Duff walked out.

Lovey Cooper had just pulled up on the other side of Duff's pump and smiled at him as he passed.

"Morning," she said.

"Morning," he said, and ducked his head.

Lovey knew everyone in town, and she didn't recognize him. And she was nosy.

"It's a bit cool this morning, isn't it?" she said.

"Yes, ma'am," Duff said, watching the numbers rolling over on the pump.

"I own Granny's Country Kitchen, and I think I saw you in there the other day."

Duff nodded. "I was there. Food's good."

Lovey smiled. "Music to my ears. Are you here visiting family for the holidays?"

"No, ma'am. We used to live here, but we're in Florida now."

"Well, I'll say. Who are your people?" Lovey asked.

"Zack and Candi Martin."

"Names are familiar, but I can't place them. Have y'all been gone long?"

Duff sighed. There was no need to hide his truth.

"About ten years. I was just a little kid when we moved, so I don't remember hardly anyone."

"So, are you here for the festivities? There's a big Christmas parade tomorrow. It starts at 10:00 a.m. If you're still here, you won't want to miss that."

Duff nodded and then his pump kicked off.

"I guess I'm done here," he said. "Nice talking to you." Then he replaced the nozzle and put the gas cap back on the car.

"See you at the parade!" Lovey said.

Duff waved, then got in the car and drove away.

Lovey watched, still trying to remember why that name was familiar. The kid was clean-cut and polite. A little skinny, but he had pretty brown hair with a tendency to curl. And she knew those names from somewhere. It would come to her later.

Her pump kicked off. She finished up and headed to Granny's. She was still standing in for one of the waitresses who'd come down with the flu, and there was no time to waste.

━━━━━━

Duff had driven by the library yesterday, and Blessings was too small to get lost in, so he found his way back with no problem. His phone dinged as he was about to get out. This time, it was a text from Allen.

Thanks for checking in. Whatever is going on,

be a man about it. Don't wind up like Dad. And

bring my car back in one piece. Love you.

Duff's eyes welled. Men admitted their mistakes. Men told the truth. He was working on both of those, but before he went to the police for help, he needed to make sure he knew what he was talking about. He got out of the car with purpose, went inside, and then straight up to the lady at the desk.

Gina Green looked up, surprised anyone was here this early and even more surprised to see a face she didn't know.

"Good morning," she said as the boy stopped at her desk.

"Morning, ma'am. Do you have back issues of the local newspaper on file?"

"Yes, we do. Are you looking for a particular story or researching?"

"A particular story."

"Do you have a date?" Gina asked.

"Not a specific date, but I know it was ten years ago...and it was in the summer, so June or July because school was out."

"Okay...what's the story about?" Gina asked.

"Zack Martin being arrested for stealing jewelry from a woman and any supporting stories afterward."

Gina nodded, opened up the link to the local paper, typed in *Zack Martin*, *arrest*, *jewelry*, and made some notes.

"This is on microfiche. If you'll follow me," Gina said, and led him to a back corner of the room and their only microfiche reader. "Just have a seat and I'll pull the film."

Duff's heart was pounding. His stomach was in knots. If that old woman hadn't passed away, then his mama would never have mentioned that name and he wouldn't have heard her and Allen talking about the details of what sent his dad to prison, and he wouldn't be here trying to right a wrong. It seemed sad that a lady had to die for him to know he'd done something wrong.

Gina came back with two small tin cylinders. "The stories regarding this arrest and the ensuing trial are in both of these. I'll load the first one for you. When you've finished, I can either load the next for you, or you're free to do it yourself. Just replace the first one in the same tin you took it out of before you remove the next."

"Yes, ma'am," Duff said, watching carefully as she loaded the film, then showed him how to use the reader.

It was awkward at first, but he soon got the hang of it and began searching.

He found the first story right off, and the photo of his

dad in handcuffs and being escorted into the courthouse for arraignment was horrifying. According to the article, his dad kept proclaiming his innocence. They couldn't prove he'd stolen the jewels, but he'd been the only member outside of the family in the house, and they discovered the jewels were missing after he left. And as Duff read, he saw his dad even had some prior offenses that weighed against him. He read it all with tears in his eyes.

He switched to the second roll of microfiche and started looking for follow-up stories. There were two. One was a story about the trial, and the second was the story about the verdict. Bottom line...his dad was in jail for something he didn't do, and Duff hoped he could prove it.

He got up with the tins of microfiche and took them up to the desk.

"Thank you for your help," he said.

Gina smiled. "Of course. Did you find everything you were looking for?"

Duff sighed "Yes, ma'am" and then left the library and went back to the car and got in.

The air-conditioning in the library hadn't been all that cold, but he was shivering. It felt like he was coming undone. A part of him regretted even hearing what his mom and brother were talking about, and at the same time, he was horrified that they'd never told him.

His stomach was protesting from the meager breakfast he'd had. Maybe if he got some food in his belly, the shaking would stop. So he started the car and drove back to Granny's. He wanted to be inside, eating real food, not premade stuff from the grocery store deli.

He couldn't help but think of the pretty woman he kept seeing as he pulled in and parked. It still felt like she was part of his story here, but he couldn't make the connection. He got out and went inside.

As soon as he was seated, he ordered coffee. Maybe that would stop the shaking. It came with a basket of biscuits. He ordered beef stew and cornbread, and then while he was waiting for his order, he began buttering biscuits and downing them like popcorn. He didn't stop until they were gone.

The hot coffee and warm food stopped the shaking, but they did nothing to ease the knot in his belly. When his food came, he buttered the cornbread, too, and then ate slowly, savoring the thick, hot stew, rife with bite-size chunks of beef, tender coins of carrots, perfectly cubed potatoes, and small slivers of onion. And as he ate, a calm came over him.

Whatever happened now just had to happen, because this was what it meant to do the right thing.

Lovey didn't wait on his table, but she saw him and came to say hello.

"Hello again, young man. How about a piece of pie on the house?"

Duff blinked. "Uh…yes, ma'am. That would be awesome."

"We have chocolate, lemon, and coconut cream pies. We also have apple and cherry pie, and peach cobbler. What's your pleasure?"

He smiled shyly. "I think I'd like some of that peach cobbler."

"Awesome choice! Do you want it à la mode or straight?"

"I never turn down ice cream," Duff said. "I'll take it à la mode."

Lovey gave him a quick pat on the shoulder.

"Coming right up," she said, and headed for the kitchen.

Duff was still smiling when the same pretty, dark-haired woman walked into the dining room, only this time she wasn't alone. She was with another woman, and they were talking and laughing as they were being seated. All he could think was this was meant to be. He wanted to talk to her, and here she was.

And then Lovey returned with dessert, and he finished off his meal, devouring the peach cobbler à la mode.

———————

Bridgette had just hung the last ornament on the Christmas tree when her sister, Emma, walked into the store. She saw Birdie and headed straight toward her.

"I didn't know y'all had Christmas ornaments! For that matter, I didn't know there was a gift shop here!" Emma said.

Bridgette nodded. "It was Wade's idea. The gift shop has been here for several months, but the ornaments are special for Christmas. What better way to advertise they are here than to see them on a tree?"

"Oh my word! You even have those cute little cast-iron pans that make sticks of cornbread look like ears of corn! I always wanted one of those. And look at the potholders and aprons! And the jars of jams and jellies. Oh my lord! Cute little dog sweaters. They have Santa Claus on them. Makes me want a dog just so I could dress it up!" Emma said.

Bridgette rolled her eyes. "About the third time you had to get up at night and let it out to pee, you'd be tired of that dog and its cute clothes."

Emma giggled. "You know me so well. Still, there are some

really nice things here. I'm going to have to come back to do a little Christmas shopping. Right now, I'm here to invite you to lunch. Can you go?"

"Yes, sure. Just let me tell Wade," Bridgette said, and left Emma poking about the gift shop as she went to look for him.

He wasn't in the office, which meant he was likely somewhere in the warehouse working on the float. She sent him a text, grabbed her purse, and went back to find Emma at the register.

"I just couldn't resist this salt-and-pepper-shaker set," Emma said. "Look, the rooster is the pepper shaker, and the hen holds the salt."

Bridgette grinned. "Awesome."

A few minutes later, they were in Emma's car and on their way to Granny's. The parking lot was filling up, and the dining room was already getting busy. Bridgette didn't see the boy again until she and Emma had already ordered, and then all of a sudden he was standing at their table.

"Ladies, I apologize for interrupting your meal, but could I talk to you for a minute?"

Emma was startled, but Bridgette was intrigued.

"Yes, if you'll explain why you've been staring at me every time we happen to cross paths," Bridgette said.

Emma frowned. "If my sister says okay, then sit, but this better be good."

"Thank you," he said, and sat in one of the empty chairs at their table. "I won't bother you but a minute. My family was from Blessings, but we moved away when I was six, so I don't remember many names."

"What's your name?" Bridgette asked.

"Duff Martin. What's yours?"

"Bridgette Knox."

"Most everyone calls her Birdie," Emma said. "I'm Emma, her older sister."

Duff's eyes widened. "Oh my gosh! Yes. Birdie. You're Miss Margie's girl! She babysat me after school! I knew you looked familiar."

Bridgette sighed. "And you're Duffy! I remember you. I think you were probably the last one she kept, and you were such a little guy."

Duff nodded. "Yes, ma'am. Would it be possible to talk to Miss Margie? She might be able to answer some questions for me."

Both Emma and Bridgette shook their heads.

"No. I'm sorry. Mama died last New Year's Day," Bridgette said.

Duff's shoulders slumped. "Aw, man…I'm sorry."

But Emma was frowning now, remembering. "Your parents were Candi and Zack, right?"

Duff nodded. "Yes, ma'am. And yes, Dad's in prison. That's part of why I'm here. There's very little I remember about that time, and I was hoping your mother would be able to fill in some blanks."

"So ask us," Bridgette said. "Emma and I always knew the children Mama kept, and they knew us."

"What do you remember about me?" he asked.

Emma thought a few moments. "You had curly hair, and you liked jigsaw puzzles. I remember seeing you and Mama working them together at the kitchen table."

Duff's eyes widened. "I'd forgotten all about jigsaw puzzles. I was obsessed with them for the longest time."

"Oh, I remember one thing," Bridgette said. "You dug holes all over the place. Mama was always having Ray or Junior—those are our brothers—filling them back up again."

Duff frowned. "I dug holes? Why was I digging holes?"

"You liked to play pirates," Emma said. "You were always begging Mama to let you watch the CD she had of *Pirates of the Caribbean*. And then you would stomp all through the house, saying 'argh' and 'ahoy, matey.' You were so cute."

Bridgette nodded. "That's why you kept digging the holes. You were looking for buried treasure. I remember one day your dad was working for a lady, and he called Mom, asking if she could come get you because he was trying to finish up this job. I was home. Mom was busy, so she sent me. When I got there, you were head down in some hole the gardener had just dug, and he was trying to plant some new rosebushes. I got you out of the hole, brushed you off, and we left. We went through the drive-through at Broyles Dairy Freeze to get ice cream before I took you to Mom's. Do you remember that?"

Duff was in shock. "Oh my God."

Bridgette frowned. "What's wrong?"

Duff just shook his head. "It's a long story, but I can't thank you enough for talking to me. I've got to go."

"Wait!" Bridgette said. "Is your family here for a visit, or by any chance are you moving back?"

"No, ma'am. We're not moving back, and thank you both again. You'll never know how much this meant to me, and it's really nice seeing you again."

He got up and hurried out.

"What in the world was that all about?" Emma asked.

Bridgette shrugged. "I don't know. I have been seeing him

around, and every time he would just stare at me. Now I know why."

"I wonder what he's doing here," Emma said.

"I have no idea," Bridgette said.

Emma shrugged it off. "Oh well, here comes our food, and what's this I've been hearing about you being on one of the floats in the Christmas parade? I heard the guys at the feed store talking about it."

"It's just advertisement for the feed store. Wade asked if I would and of course I agreed."

"What fun!" Emma said. "I wish I was going to be in the parade."

Bridgette grinned, thinking about the mechanical bull.

"I'll wave at you," she said, popped a french fry in her mouth, then reached for the salt.

About the Author

Carolyn Brown is a *New York Times*, *USA Today*, *Wall Street Journal*, *Publishers Weekly* and #1 Amazon and #1 *Washington Post* bestselling author and a RITA finalist. She is the author of more than one hundred novels and several novellas. She's a recipient of the Bookseller's Best Award and the prestigious Montlake Diamond Award, and also a three-time recipient of the National Readers Choice Award. Brown has been published for more than twenty years, and her books have been translated into twenty foreign languages.

She's been married for more than fifty years to Mr. B, and they have three smart, wonderful, amazing children; fifteen grandchildren; and too many great-grands to keep track of. When she's not writing, she likes to plot new stories in her backyard with her tomcat, Boots Randolph Terminator

Outlaw, who protects the yard from all kinds of wicked var-mints like crickets, locusts, and spiders.

Carolyn can be found on Instagram @carolynbrownbooks, on Twitter @thecarolynbrown, on Facebook at facebook.com /carolynbrownbooks, and at her website, carolynlbrown.com.

THE HONEYMOON INN

New York Times bestselling author Carolyn
Brown's Texas twang and inimitable sass shine
as close proximity leads to a fiery fling

Pearl Richland left home as soon as she could and never thought
she'd look back. And she didn't, until she lost her job at the bank
and had to fall back on the only thing left to her name: the motel
her great-aunt Pearlita left to her. But with a winter storm coming
and some suspicious activity around town, Pearl hunkers down in
the motel with the only guest passing through town, a man named
Will Marshall. Luckily, he's a welcome distraction as the long, cold
days quickly turn to hot nights…

Previously published as *Red's Hot Cowboy*.

**"[A] fresh, funny, and sexy tale filled with
likable, down-to-earth characters."**

—*Booklist* for *Love Drunk Cowboy*

For more info about Sourcebooks's books and authors, visit:

sourcebooks.com

WELCOME BACK TO RAMBLING, TEXAS

From acclaimed author June Faver: the women of Rambling tackle small-town living in the heart of Texas Hill Country

Reggie Lee Stafford is a hometown girl living in Rambling, the small Texas town where she was born. As a single mother, her world revolves around her young daughter and her beloved job at the local newspaper. But her peaceful life is turned upside down when Frank Bell—the bane of Reggie's teenage existence—returns to town to claim his vast inheritance.

"June Faver is a must-read author."

—*Harlequin Junkie*

HOPE ON THE RANGE

Welcome to the Turn Around Ranch:
charming contemporary cowboy romance from
USA Today bestselling author Cindi Madsen

Brady Dawson has been in love with Tanya Greer for as long as he can remember. But running the Turn Around Ranch with his family doesn't leave much downtime for relationships. Now that Tanya is contemplating a move to the city, it looks like he might never get his chance... Faced with the realization that he might lose Tanya forever, he'll have to cowboy up and prove to Tanya that the Turn Around Ranch is the perfect place to call home.

"Feel-good romance...full of witty charm."

—A. J. Pine, *USA Today* bestselling author

For more info about Sourcebooks's books and authors, visit:

sourcebooks.com

MAGNOLIA BAY MEMORIES

Welcome to Magnolia Bay, a heartwarming series with
a Southern flair from author Babette de Jongh

Director Heather Gabriel and business consultant Adrian Crawford
are on a mission to help Bayside Barn on their latest project. Both
Heather and Adrian have some grieving and growing to do before
they'll be ready for love, but when they're together, all their other
worries fly away. Meanwhile, Charlie—a horse who blames himself
for his beloved human's death—learns to heal and teaches them a
lesson about unconditional love.

**"De Jongh's Magnolia Bay series charms with just
the right blend of romance and animal cameos."**

—Debbie Burns

For more info about Sourcebooks's books and authors, visit:

sourcebooks.com

THAT DEEP RIVER FEELING

Romance has an Alaska homecoming in this
bold, sexy series from Jackie Ashenden

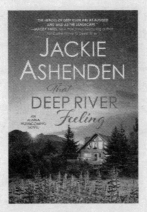

Zeke Calhoun doesn't care much about Deep River, but he'll do just
about anything to keep the last promise he made—to look out for
his best friend's sister.

As the sole police officer in Deep River, Morgan West won't
be bossed around, but Zeke is irresistible. He's tough, challeng-
ing, and all kinds of sexy, but getting involved is the last thing on
Morgan's mind...

**"The heroes of Deep River are as rugged
and wild as the landscape."**

—Maisey Yates, *New York Times* bestselling author

For more info about Sourcebooks's books and authors, visit:

sourcebooks.com

Also by Carolyn Brown